THE SEVEN VOYAGES OF SINBAD THE SAILOR

Translated by Sir Richard Burton

A Digireads.com Book
Digireads.com Publishing

The Seven Voyages of Sinbad the Sailor
By Anonymous
Translated by Sir Richard Burton
ISBN: 1-4209-3195-4

Please visit *www.digireads.com*

CONTENTS

THE SEVEN VOYAGES OF SINBAD THE SAILOR

Note on the Text

The following text has been drawn from Sir Richard Burton's exhaustive translation of *The Book of the Thousand Nights and a Night*, more commonly known as *The Arabian Nights*. Throughout the body of the text, the spelling of "Sinbad" has been retained as "Sindbad" as it originally appeared and has only been changed in the title to represent the more modern spelling that most readers will be commonly familiar with. The text is presented in its original and uncensored format and as such may not be suitable for younger readers.

SINDBAD THE SEAMAN [1]
AND SINDBAD THE LANDSMAN.

There lived in the city of Baghdad, during the reign of the Commander
of the Faithful, Harun al-Rashid, a man named Sindbád the Hammál,
[2] one in poor case who bore burdens on his head for hire. It happened
to him one day of great heat that whilst he was carrying a heavy load,
he became exceeding weary and sweated profusely, the heat and the
weight alike oppressing him. Presently, as he was passing the gate of a
merchant's house, before which the ground was swept and watered, and
there the air was temperate, he sighted a broad bench beside the door;
so he set his load thereon, to take rest and smell the air,—And
Shahrazad perceived the dawn of day and ceased saying her permitted
say.

When it was the Five Hundred and Thirty-seventh Night,

She said, It hath reached me, O auspicious King, that when the Hammal
set his load upon the bench to take rest and smell the air, there came out
upon him from the court-door a pleasant breeze and a delicious
fragrance. He sat down on the edge of the bench, and at once heard
from within the melodious sound of lutes and other stringed
instruments, and mirth-exciting voices singing and reciting, together
with the song of birds warbling and glorifying Almighty Allah in
various tunes and tongues; turtles, mocking-birds, merles, nightingales,
cushats and stone-curlews, [3] whereat he marvelled in himself and was
moved to mighty joy and solace. Then he went up to the gate and saw
within a great flower-garden wherein were pages and black slaves and
such a train of servants and attendants and so forth as is found only
with Kings and Sultans; and his nostrils were greeted with the savoury
odours of all manner meats rich and delicate, and delicious and
generous wines. So he raised his eyes heavenwards and said, "Glory to
Thee, O Lord, O Creator and Provider, who providest whomso Thou
wilt without count or stint! O mine Holy One, I cry Thee pardon for all
sins and turn to Thee repenting of all offences! O Lord, there is no
gainsaying Thee in Thine ordinance and Thy dominion, neither wilt
Thou be questioned of that Thou dost, for Thou indeed over all things
art Almighty! Extolled be Thy perfection: whom Thou wilt Thou
makest poor and whom Thou wilt Thou makest rich! Whom Thou wilt
Thou exaltest and whom Thou wilt Thou abasest and there is no god
but Thou! How mighty is Thy majesty and how enduring Thy

dominion and how excellent Thy government! Verily, Thou favourest whom Thou wilt of Thy servants, whereby the owner of this place abideth in all joyance of life and delighteth himself with pleasant scents and delicious meats and exquisite wines of all kinds. For indeed Thou appointest unto Thy creatures that which Thou wilt and that which Thou hast foreordained unto them; wherefore are some weary and others are at rest and some enjoy fair fortune and affluence, whilst others suffer the extreme of travail and misery, even as I do." And he fell to reciting,

"How many by my labours, that evermore endure,
All goods of life enjoy and in cooly shade recline?
Each morn that dawns I wake in travail and in woe,
And strange is my condition and my burden gars me pine:
Many others are in luck and from miseries are free,
And Fortune never loads them with loads the like o' mine:
They live their happy days in all solace and delight;
Eat, drink and dwell in honour 'mid the noble and the digne:
All living things were made of a little drop of sperm,
Thine origin is mine and my provenance is thine;
Yet the difference and distance 'twixt the twain of us are far
As the difference of savour 'twixt vinegar and wine:
But at Thee, O God All-wise! I venture not to rail
Whose ordinance is just and whose justice cannot fail."

When Sindbad the Porter had made an end of reciting his verses, he bore up his burden and was about to fare on, when there came forth to him from the gate a little foot-page, fair of face and shapely of shape and dainty of dress who caught him by the hand saying, "Come in and speak with my lord, for he calleth for thee." The Porter would have excused himself to the page but the lad would take no refusal; so he left his load with the doorkeeper in the vestibule and followed the boy into the house, which he found to be a goodly mansion, radiant and full of majesty, till he brought him to a grand sitting-room wherein he saw a company of nobles and great lords, seated at tables garnished with all manner of flowers and sweet-scented herbs, besides great plenty of dainty viands and fruits dried and fresh and confections and wines of the choicest vintages. There also were instruments of music and mirth and lovely slave-girls playing and singing. All the company was ranged according to rank; and in the highest place sat a man of worshipful and noble aspect whose beard-sides hoariness had stricken; and he was stately of stature and fair of favour, agreeable of aspect and full of gravity and dignity and majesty. So Sindbad the Porter was confounded at that which he beheld and said in himself, "By Allah, this must be either a piece of Paradise or some King's palace!" Then he saluted the company with much respect praying for their prosperity, and kissing the ground before them, stood with his head bowed down in humble attitude.—And Shahrazad perceived the dawn of day and ceased to say her permitted say.

When it was the Five Hundred and Thirty-eighth Night,

She said, It hath reached me, O auspicious King, that Sindbad the Porter, after kissing ground between their hands stood with his head bowed down in humble attitude. The master of the house bade him draw near and be seated and bespoke him kindly, bidding him welcome. Then he set before him various kinds of viands, rich and delicate and delicious, and the Porter, after saying his Bismillah, fell to and ate his fill, after which he exclaimed, "Praised be Allah whatso be our case! [4]" and, washing his hands, returned thanks to the company for his entertainment. Quoth the host, "Thou art welcome and thy day is a blessed. But what is thy name and calling?" Quoth the other, "O my lord, my name is Sindbad the Hammal, and I carry folk's goods on my head for hire." The house-master smiled and rejoined, "Know, O Porter that thy name is even as mine, for I am Sindbad the Seaman; and now, O Porter, I would have thee let me hear the couplets thou recitedst at the gate anon." The Porter was abashed and replied, "Allah upon thee! Excuse me, for toil and travail and lack of luck when the hand is empty, teach a man ill manners and boorish ways." Said the host, "Be not ashamed; thou art become my brother; but repeat to me the verses, for they pleased me whenas I heard thee recite them at the gate. Hereupon the Porter repeated the couplets and they delighted the merchant, who said to him, "Know, O Hammal, that my story is a wonderful one, and thou shalt hear all that befel me and all I underwent ere I rose to this state of prosperity and became the lord of this place wherein thou seest me; for I came not to this high estate save after travail sore and perils galore, and how much toil and trouble have I not suffered in days of yore! I have made seven voyages, by each of which hangeth a marvellous tale, such as confoundeth the reason, and all this came to pass by doom of fortune and fate; for from what destiny doth write there is neither refuge nor flight. Know, then, good my lords (continued he) that I am about to relate the

THE FIRST VOYAGE OF SINDBAD THE SEAMAN. [5]

My father was a merchant, one of the notables of my native place, a monied man and ample of means, who died whilst I was yet a child, leaving me much wealth in money and lands and farmhouses. When I grew up, I laid hands on the whole and ate of the best and drank freely and wore rich clothes and lived lavishly, companioning and consorting with youths of my own age, and considering that this course of life would continue for ever and ken no change. Thus did I for a long time, but at last I awoke from my heedlessness and, returning to my senses, I found my wealth had become unwealth and my condition ill-conditioned and all I once hent had left my hand. And recovering my reason I was stricken with dismay and confusion and bethought me of a saying of our lord Solomon, son of David (on whom be peace!), which I had heard aforetime from my father, "Three things are better than other three; the day of death is better than the day of birth, a live dog is better than a dead lion and the grave is better than want." [6] Then I got together my remains of estates and property and sold all, even my clothes, for three thousand dirhams, with which I resolved to travel to foreign parts, remembering the saying of the poet,

"By means of toil man shall scale the height;
Who to fame aspires mustn't sleep o' night:
Who seeketh pearl in the deep must dive,
Winning weal and wealth by his main and might:
And who seeketh Fame without toil and strife
Th' impossible seeketh and wasteth life."

So taking heart I bought me goods, merchandise and all needed for a voyage and, impatient to be at sea, I embarked, with a company of merchants, on board a ship bound for Bassorah. There we again embarked and sailed many days and nights, and we passed from isle to isle and sea to sea and shore to shore, buying and selling and bartering everywhere the ship touched, and continued our course till we came to an island as it were a garth of the gardens of Paradise. Here the captain cast anchor and making fast to the shore, put out the landing planks. So all on board landed and made furnaces [7] and lighting fires therein, busied themselves in various ways, some cooking and some washing, whilst other some walked about the island for solace, and the crew fell to eating and drinking and playing and sporting. I was one of the walkers but, as we were thus engaged, behold the master who was standing on the gunwale cried out to us at the top of his voice, saying, "Ho there! passengers, run for your lives and hasten back to the ship and leave your gear and save yourselves from destruction, Allah preserve you! For this island whereon ye stand is no true island, but a great fish stationary a-middlemost of the sea, whereon the sand hath settled and trees have sprung up of old time, so that it is become like unto an island; [8] but, when ye lighted fires on it, it felt the heat and moved; and in a moment it will sink with you into the sea and ye will all be drowned. So leave your gear and seek your safety ere ye die!"— And Shahrazad perceived the dawn of day and ceased saying her permitted say.

When it was the Five Hundred and Thirty-ninth Night,

She said, It hath reached me, O auspicious King, that when the ship-master cried to the passengers, "Leave your gear and seek safety, ere ye die;" all who heard him left gear and goods, clothes washed and unwashed, fire pots and brass cooking-pots, and fled back to the ship for their lives, and some reached it while others (amongst whom was I) did not, for suddenly the island shook and sank into the abysses of the deep, with all that were thereon, and the dashing sea surged over it with clashing waves. I sank with the others down, down into the deep, but Almighty Allah preserved me from drowning and threw in my way a great wooden tub of those that had served the ship's company for tubbing. I gripped it for the sweetness of life and, bestriding it like one riding, paddled with my feet like oars, whilst the waves tossed me as in sport right and left. Meanwhile the captain made sail and departed with those who had reached the ship, regardless of the drowning and the drowned; and I ceased not following the vessel with my eyes, till she was hid from sight and I made sure of death. Darkness closed in upon me while in this plight and the winds and waves bore me on all that night and the next day, till the tub brought to with me under the lee of a lofty island, with trees overhanging the tide. I caught hold of a branch and by its aid clambered up on to the land, after coming nigh upon death; but when I reached the shore, I found my legs cramped and numbed and my feet bore traces of the nibbling of fish upon their soles; withal I had felt nothing for excess of anguish and fatigue. I threw myself down on the island ground, like a dead man, and drowned in desolation swooned away, nor did I return to my senses till next morning, when the sun rose and revived me. But I found my feet swollen, so made shift to move by shuffling on my breech and crawling on my knees, for in that island were found store of fruits and springs of sweet water. I ate of the fruits which strengthened me; and thus I abode days and nights, till my life seemed to return and my spirits began to revive and I was better able to move about. So, after due consideration, I fell to exploring the island and diverting myself with gazing upon all things that Allah Almighty had created there; and rested under the trees from one of which I cut me a staff to lean upon. One day as I walked along the marge, I caught sight of some object in the distance and thought it a wild beast or one of the monster-creatures of the sea; but, as I drew near it, looking hard the while, I saw that it was a noble mare, tethered on the beach. Presently I went up to her, but she cried out against me with a great cry, so that I trembled for fear and turned to go away, when there came forth a man from under the earth and followed me, crying out and saying, "Who and whence art thou, and what caused thee to come hither?" "O my lord," answered I, "I am in very sooth, a waif, a stranger, and was left to drown with sundry others by the ship we voyaged in; [9] but Allah graciously sent me a wooden tub; so I saved myself thereon and it floated with me, till the waves cast me up on this island." When he heard this, he took my hand and saying, "Come with me," carried me into a great Sardab, or underground chamber, which was spacious as a saloon. He made me sit down at its upper end; then he brought me somewhat of food and, being anhungered, I ate till I was satisfied and refreshed; and when he had put me at mine ease he questioned me of myself, and I told him all that had befallen me from first to last; and, as he wondered at my adventure, I said, "By Allah, O my lord, excuse me; I have told thee the truth of my case and the accident which betided me; and now I desire that thou tell me who thou art and why thou abidest here under the earth and why thou hast tethered yonder mare on the brink of the sea." Answered he, "Know, that I am one of the several who are stationed in different parts of this island, and we are of the grooms of King Mihrjan [10] and under our hand are all his horses. Every month, about new-moon tide we bring hither our best mares which have never been covered, and picket them on the sea-shore and hide ourselves in this place under the ground, so that none may espy us. Presently, the stallions of the sea scent the mares and come up out of the water and seeing no one, leap the mares and do their will of them. When they have covered them, they try to drag them away with them, but cannot, by reason of the leg-ropes; so they cry out at them and butt at them and kick them, which we hearing, know that the stallions have dismounted; so we run out and shout at them, whereupon they are startled and return in fear to the sea. Then the mares conceive by them and bear colts and fillies worth a mint of money, nor is their like to be found on earth's face. This is the time of the coming forth of the sea-stallions; and Inshallah! I will bear thee to King Mihrjan"—And Shahrazad perceived the dawn of day and ceased to say her permitted say.

When it was the Five Hundred and Fortieth Night,

She continued, It hath reached me, O auspicious King, that the Syce [11] said to Sindbad the Seaman, "I will bear thee to King Mihrjan and show thee our country. And know that hadst thou not happened on us thou hadst perished miserably and none had known of thee: but I will be the means of the saving of thy life and of thy return to thine own land." I called down blessings on him and thanked him for his kindness and courtesy; and, while we were yet talking, behold, the stallion came up out of the sea; and, giving a great cry, sprang upon the mare and covered her. When he had done his will of her, he dismounted and would have carried her away with him, but could not by reason of the tether. She kicked and cried out at him, whereupon the groom took a sword and target [12] and ran out of the underground saloon, smiting the buckler with the blade and calling to his company, who came up shouting and brandishing spears; and the stallion took fright at them and plunging into the sea, like a buffalo, disappeared under the waves. [13] After this we sat awhile, till the rest of the grooms came up, each leading a mare, and seeing me with their fellow-Syce, questioned me of my case and I repeated my story to them. Thereupon they drew near me and spreading the table, ate and invited me to eat; so I ate with them, after which they took horse and mounting me on one of the mares, set out with me and fared on without ceasing, till we came to the capital city of King Mihrjan, and going in to him acquainted him with my story. Then he sent for me, and when they set me before him and salams had been exchanged, he gave me a cordial welcome and wishing me long life bade me tell him my tale. So I related to him all that I had seen and all that had befallen me from first to last, whereat he marvelled and said to me, "By Allah, O my son, thou hast indeed been miraculously preserved! Were not the term of thy life a long one, thou hadst not escaped from these straits; but praised by Allah for safety!" Then he spoke cheerily to me and entreated me with kindness and consideration: moreover, he made me his agent for the port and registrar of all ships that entered the harbour. I attended him regularly, to receive his commandments, and he favoured me and did me all manner of kindness and invested me with costly and splendid robes. Indeed, I was high in credit with him, as an intercessor for the folk and an intermediary between them and him, when they wanted aught of him. I abode thus a great while and, as often as I passed through the city to the port, I questioned the merchants and travellers and sailors of the city of Baghdad; so haply I might hear of an occasion to return to my native land, but could find none who knew it or knew any who resorted thither. At this I was chagrined, for I was weary of long strangerhood; and my disappointment endured for a time till one day, going in to King Mihrjan, I found him with a company of Indians. I saluted them and they returned my salam; and politely welcomed me and asked me of my country.—And Shahrazad perceived the dawn of day and ceased saying her permitted say.

When it was the Five Hundred and Forty-first Night,

She continued, It hath reached me, O auspicious King, that Sindbad the Seaman said:—When they asked me of my country I questioned them of theirs and they told me that they were of various castes, some being called Shakiriyah [14] who are the noblest of their castes and neither oppress nor offer violence to any, and others Brahmans, a folk who abstain from wine, but live in delight and solace and merriment and own camels and horses and cattle. Moreover, they told me that the people of India are divided into two-and-seventy castes, and I marvelled at this with exceeding marvel. Amongst other things that I saw in King Mihrjan's dominions was an island called Kásil, [15] wherein all night is heard the beating of drums and tabrets; but we were told by the neighbouring islanders and by travellers that the inhabitants are people of diligence and judgment. [16] In this sea I saw also a fish two hundred cubits long and the fishermen fear it; so they strike together pieces of wood and put it to flight. [17] I also saw another fish, with a head like that of an owl, besides many other wonders and rarities, which it would be tedious to recount. I occupied myself thus in visiting the islands till, one day, as I stood in the port, with a staff in my hand, according to my custom, behold, a great ship, wherein were many merchants, came sailing for the harbour. When it reached the small inner port where ships anchor under the city, the master furled his sails and making fast to the shore, put out the landing-planks, whereupon the crew fell to breaking bulk and landing cargo whilst I stood by, taking written note of them. They were long in bringing the goods ashore so I asked the master, "Is there aught left in thy ship?"; and he answered, "O my lord, there are divers bales of merchandise in the hold, whose owner was drowned from amongst us at one of the islands on our course; so his goods remained in our charge by way of trust and we purpose to sell them and note their price, that we may convey it to his people in the city of Baghdad, the Home of Peace." "What was the merchant's name?" quoth I, and quoth he, "Sindbad the Seaman;" whereupon I straitly considered him and knowing him, cried out to him with a great cry, saying, "O captain, I am that Sindbad the Seaman who travelled with other merchants; and when the fish heaved and thou calledst to us some saved themselves and others sank, I being one of them. But Allah Almighty threw in my way a great tub of wood, of those the crew had used to wash withal, and the winds and waves carried me to this island, where by Allah's grace, I fell in with King Mihrjan's grooms and they brought me hither to the King their master. When I told him my story, he entreated me with favour and made me his harbour-master, and I have prospered in his service and found acceptance with him. These bales, therefore are mine, the goods which God hath given me."—And Shahrazad perceived the dawn of day and ceased to say her permitted say.

When it was the Five Hundred and Forty-second Night,

She continued, It hath reached me, O auspicious King, that when Sindbad the Seaman said to the captain, "These bales are mine, the goods which Allah hath given me," the other exclaimed, "There is no Majesty and there is no Might save in Allah, the Glorious, the Great! Verily, there is neither conscience nor good faith left among men!" said I, "O Rais, [18] what mean these words, seeing that I have told thee my case?" And he answered, "Because thou heardest me say that I had with me goods whose owner was drowned, thou thinkest to take them without right; but this is forbidden by law to thee, for we saw him drown before our eyes, together with many other passengers, nor was one of them saved. So how canst thou pretend that thou art the owner of the goods?" "O captain," said I, "listen to my story and give heed to my words, and my truth will be manifest to thee; for lying and leasing are the letter-marks of the hypocrites." Then I recounted to him all that had befallen me since I sailed from Baghdad with him to the time when we came to the fish-island where we were nearly drowned; and I reminded him of certain matters which had passed between us; whereupon both he and the merchants were certified at the truth of my story and recognized me and gave me joy of my deliverance, saying, "By Allah, we thought not that thou hadst escaped drowning! But the Lord hath granted thee new life." Then they delivered my bales to me, and I found my name written thereon, nor was aught thereof lacking. So I opened them and making up a present for King Mihrjan of the finest and costliest of the contents, caused the sailors carry it up to the palace, where I went in to the King and laid my present at his feet, acquainting him with what had happened, especially concerning the ship and my goods; whereat he wondered with exceeding wonder and the truth of all that I had told him was made manifest to him. His affection for me redoubled after that and he showed me exceeding honour and bestowed on me a great present in return for mine. Then I sold my bales and what other matters I owned making a great profit on them, and bought me other goods and gear of the growth and fashion of the island-city. When the merchants were about to start on their homeward voyage, I embarked on board the ship all that I possessed, and going in to the King, thanked him for all his favours and friendship and craved his leave to return to my own land and friends. He farewelled me and bestowed on me great store of the country-stuffs and produce; and I took leave of him and embarked. Then we set sail and fared on nights and days, by the permission of Allah Almighty; and Fortune served us and Fate favoured us, so that we arrived in safety at Bassorah-city where I landed rejoiced at my safe return to my natal soil. After a short stay, I set out for Baghdad, the House of Peace, with store of goods and commodities of great price. Reaching the city in due time, I went straight to my own quarter and entered my house where all my friends and kinsfolk came to greet me. Then I bought me eunuchs and concubines, servants and negro slaves till I had a large establishment, and I bought me houses, and lands and gardens, till I was richer and in better case than before, and returned to enjoy the society of my friends and familiars more assiduously than ever, forgetting all I had suffered of fatigue and hardship and strangerhood and every peril of travel; and I applied myself to all manner joys and solaces and delights, eating the daintiest viands and drinking the deliciousest wines; and my wealth allowed this state of things to endure. "This, then, is the story of my first voyage, and to-morrow, Inshallah! I will tell you the tale of the second of my seven voyages." (Saith he who telleth the tale), Then Sindbad the Seaman made Sindbad the Landsman sup with him and bade give him an hundred gold pieces, saying, "Thou hast cheered us with thy company this day." [19] The Porter thanked him and, taking the gift, went his way, pondering that which he had heard and marvelling mightily at what things betide mankind. He passed the night in his own place and with early morning repaired to the abode of Sindbad the Seaman, who received him with honour and seated him by his side. As soon as the rest of the company was assembled, he set meat and drink before them and, when they had well eaten and drunken and were merry and in cheerful case, he took up his discourse and recounted to them in these words the narrative of

THE SECOND VOYAGE OF SINDBAD THE SEAMAN.

Know, O my brother, that I was living a most comfortable and enjoyable life, in all solace and delight, as I told you yesterday,—And Shahrazad perceived the dawn of day and ceased saying her permitted say.

When it was the Five Hundred and Forty-third Night,

She continued, It hath reached me, O auspicious King, that when Sindbad the Seaman's guests were all gathered together he thus bespake them:—I was living a most enjoyable life until one day my mind became possessed with the thought of travelling about the world of men and seeing their cities and islands; and a longing seized me to traffic and to make money by trade. Upon this resolve I took a great store of cash and, buying goods and gear fit for travel, bound them up in bales. Then I went down to the river-bank, where I found a noble ship and brand-new about to sail, equipped with sails of fine cloth and well manned and provided; so I took passage in her, with a number of other merchants, and after embarking our goods we weighed anchor the same day. Right fair was our voyage and we sailed from place to place and from isle to isle; and whenever we anchored we met a crowd of merchants and notables and customers, and we took to buying and selling and bartering. At last Destiny brought us to an island, fair and verdant, in trees abundant, with yellow-ripe fruits luxuriant, and flowers fragrant and birds warbling soft descant; and streams crystalline and radiant; but no sign of man showed to the descrier, no, not a blower of the fire. [20] The captain made fast with us to this island, and the merchants and sailors landed and walked about, enjoying the shade of the trees and the song of the birds, that chanted the praises of the One, the Victorious, and marvelling at the works of the Omnipotent King. [21] I landed with the rest; and, sitting down by a spring of sweet water that welled up among the trees, took out some vivers I had with me and ate of that which Allah Almighty had allotted unto me. And so sweet was the zephyr and so fragrant were the flowers, that presently I waxed drowsy and, lying down in that place, was soon drowned in sleep. When I awoke, I found myself alone, for the ship had sailed and left me behind, nor had one of the merchants or sailors bethought himself of me. I seared the island right and left, but found neither man nor Jinn, whereat I was beyond measure troubled and my gall was like to burst for stress of chagrin and anguish and concern, because I was left quite alone, without aught of worldly gear or meat or drink, weary and heart-broken. So I gave myself up for lost and said, "Not always doth the crock escape the shock. I was saved the first time by finding one who brought me from the desert island to an inhabited place, but now there is no hope for me." Then I fell to weeping and wailing and gave myself up to an access of rage, blaming myself for having again ventured upon the perils and hardships of voyage, whenas I was at my ease in mine own house in mine own land, taking my pleasure with good meat and good drink and good clothes and lacking nothing, neither money nor goods. And I repented me of having left Baghdad, and this the more after all the travails and dangers I had undergone in my first voyage, wherein I had so narrowly escaped destruction, and exclaimed "Verily we are Allah's and unto Him we are returning!" I was indeed even as one mad and Jinn-struck and presently I rose and walked about the island, right and left and every whither, unable for trouble to sit or tarry in any one place. Then I climbed a tall tree and looked in all directions, but saw nothing save sky and sea and trees and birds and isles and sands. However, after a while my eager glances fell upon some great white thing, afar off in the interior of the island; so I came down from the tree and made for that which I had seen; and behold, it was a huge white dome rising high in air and of vast compass. I walked all around it, but found no door thereto, nor could I muster strength or nimbleness by reason of its exceeding smoothness and slipperiness. So I marked the spot where I stood and went round about the dome to measure its circumference which I found fifty good paces. And as I stood, casting about how to gain an entrance the day being near its fall and the sun being near the horizon, behold, the sun was suddenly hidden from me and the air became dull and dark. Methought a cloud had come over the sun, but it was the season of summer; so I marvelled at this and lifting my head looked steadfastly at the sky, when I saw that the cloud was none other than an enormous bird, of gigantic girth and inordinately wide of wing which, as it flew through the air, veiled the sun and hid it from the island. At this sight my wonder redoubled and I remembered a story,—And Shahrazad perceived the dawn of day and ceased to say her permitted say.

When it was the Five Hundred and Forty-fourth Night,

She said, It hath reached me, O auspicious King, that Sindbad the Seaman continued in these words:—My wonder redoubled and I remembered a story I had heard aforetime of pilgrims and travellers, how in a certain island dwelleth a huge bird, called the "Rukh" [22] which feedeth its young on elephants; and I was certified that the dome which caught my sight was none other than a Rukh's egg. As I looked and wondered at the marvellous works of the Almighty, the bird alighted on the dome and brooded over it with its wings covering it and its legs stretched out behind it on the ground, and in this posture it fell asleep, glory be to Him who sleepeth not! When I saw this, I arose and, unwinding my turband from my head, doubled it and twisted it into a rope, with which I girt my middle and bound my waist fast to the legs of the Rukh, saying in myself, "Peradventure, this bird may carry me to a land of cities and inhabitants, and that will be better than abiding in this desert island." I passed the night watching and fearing to sleep, lest the bird should fly away with me unawares; and, as soon as the dawn broke and morn shone, the Rukh rose off its egg and spreading its wings with a great cry flew up into the air dragging me with it; nor ceased it to soar and to tower till I thought it had reached the limit of the firmament; after which it descended, earthwards, little by little, till it lighted on the top of a high hill. As soon as I found myself on the hard ground, I made haste to unbind myself, quaking for fear of the bird, though it took no heed of me nor even felt me; and, loosing my turband from its feet, I made off with my best speed. Presently, I saw it catch up in its huge claws something from the earth and rise with it high in air, and observing it narrowly I saw it to be a serpent big of bulk and gigantic of girth, wherewith it flew away clean out of sight. I marvelled at this and faring forwards found myself on a peak overlooking a valley, exceeding great and wide and deep, and bounded by vast mountains that spired high in air: none could descry their summits, for the excess of their height, nor was any able to climb up thereto. When I saw this, I blamed myself for that which I had done and said, "Would Heaven I had tarried in the island! It was better than this wild desert; for there I had at least fruits to eat and water to drink, and here are neither trees nor fruits nor streams. But there is no Majesty and there is no Might save in Allah, the Glorious, the Great! Verily, as often as I am quit of one peril, I fall into a worse danger and a more grievous." However, I took courage and walking along the Wady found that its soil was of diamond, the stone wherewith they pierce minerals and precious stones and porcelain and the onyx, for that it is a dense stone and a dure, whereon neither iron nor hardhead hath effect, neither can we cut off aught therefrom nor break it, save by means of leadstone. [23] Moreover, the valley swarmed with snakes and vipers, each big as a palm tree, that would have made but one gulp of an elephant; and they came out by night, hiding during the day, lest the Rukhs and eagles pounce on them and tear them to pieces, as was their wont, why I wot not. And I repented of what I had done and said, "By Allah, I have made haste to bring destruction upon myself!" The day began to wane as I went along and I looked about for a place where I might pass the night, being in fear of the serpents; and I took no thought of meat and drink in my concern for my life. Presently, I caught sight of a cave nearhand, with a narrow doorway; so I entered and seeing a great stone close to the mouth, I rolled it up and stopped the entrance, saying to myself, "I am safe here for the night; and as soon as it is day, I will go forth and see what destiny will do." Then I looked within the cave and saw to the upper end a great serpent brooding on her eggs, at which my flesh quaked and my hair stood on end; but I raised my eyes to Heaven and, committing my case to fate and lot, abode all that night without sleep till daybreak, when I rolled back the stone from the mouth of the cave and went forth, staggering like a drunken man and giddy with watching and fear and hunger. As in this sore case I walked along the valley, behold, there fell down before me a slaughtered beast; but I saw no one, whereat I marvelled with great marvel and presently remembered a story I had heard aforetime of traders and pilgrims and travellers; how the mountains where are the diamonds are full of perils and terrors, nor can any fare through them; but the merchants who traffic in diamonds have a device by which they obtain them, that is to say, they take a sheep and slaughter and skin it and cut it in pieces and cast them down from the mountain-tops into the valley-sole, where the meat being fresh and sticky with blood, some of the gems cleave to it. There they leave it till mid-day, when the eagles and vultures swoop down upon it and carry it in their claws to the mountain-summits, whereupon the merchants come and shout at them and scare them away from the meat. Then they come and, taking the diamonds which they find sticking to it, go their ways with them and leave the meat to the birds and beasts; nor can any come at the diamonds but by this device,—And Shahrazad perceived the dawn of day and ceased saying her permitted say.

When it was the Five Hundred and Forty-fifth Night,

She said, it hath reached me, O auspicious King, that Sindbad the Seaman continued his relation of what befel him in the Mountain of Diamonds, and informed them that the merchants cannot come at the diamonds save by the device aforesaid. So, when I saw the slaughtered beast fall (he pursued) and bethought me of the story, I went up to it and filled my pockets and shawl-girdle and turband and the folds of my clothes with the choicest diamonds; and, as I was thus engaged, down fell before me another great piece of meat. Then with my unrolled turband and lying on my back, I set the bit on my breast so that I was hidden by the meat, which was thus raised above the ground. Hardly had I gripped it, when an eagle swooped down upon the flesh and, seizing it with his talons, flew up with it high in air and me clinging thereto, and ceased not its flight till it alighted on the head of one of the mountains where, dropping the carcass he fell to rending it; but, behold, there arose behind him a great noise of shouting and clattering of wood, whereat the bird took fright and flew away. Then I loosed off myself the meat, with clothes daubed with blood therefrom, and stood up by its side; whereupon up came the merchant, who had cried out at the eagle, and seeing me standing there, bespoke me not, but was affrighted at me and shook with fear. However, he went up to the carcass and turning it over, found no diamonds sticking to it, whereat he gave a great cry and exclaimed, "Harrow, my disappointment! There is no Majesty and there is no Might save in Allah with whom we seek refuge from Satan the stoned!" And he bemoaned himself and beat hand upon hand, saying, "Alas, the pity of it! How cometh this?" Then I went up to him and he said to me, "Who art thou and what causeth thee to come hither?" And I, "Fear not, I am a man and a good man and a merchant. My story is a wondrous and my adventures marvellous and the manner of my coming hither is prodigious. So be of good cheer, thou shalt receive of me what shall rejoice thee, for I have with me great plenty of diamonds and I will give thee thereof what shall suffice thee; for each is better than aught thou couldst get otherwise. So fear nothing." The man rejoiced thereat and thanked and blessed me; then we talked together till the other merchants, hearing me in discourse with their fellow, came up and saluted me; for each of them had thrown down his piece of meat. And as I went off with them I told them my whole story, how I had suffered hardships at sea and the fashion of my reaching the valley. But I gave the owner of the meat a number of the stones I had by me, so they all wished me joy of my escape, saying, "By Allah a new life hath been decreed to thee, for none ever reached yonder valley and came off thence alive before thee; but praised be Allah for thy safety!" We passed the night together in a safe and pleasant place, beyond measure rejoiced at my deliverance from the Valley of Serpents and my arrival in an inhabited land; and on the morrow we set out and journeyed over the mighty range of mountains, seeing many serpents in the valley, till we came to a fair great island, wherein was a garden of huge camphor trees under each of which an hundred men might take shelter. When the folk have a mind to get camphor, they bore into the upper part of the bole with a long iron; whereupon the liquid camphor, which is the sap of the tree, floweth out and they catch it in vessels, where it concreteth like gum; but, after this, the tree dieth and becometh firewood. [24] Moreover, there is in this island a kind of wild beast, called "Rhinoceros," [25] that pastureth as do steers and buffalos with us; but it is a huge brute, bigger of body than the camel and like it feedeth upon the leaves and twigs of trees. It is a remarkable animal with a great and thick horn, ten cubits long, amiddleward its head; wherein, when cleft in twain, is the likeness of a man. Voyagers and pilgrims and travellers declare that this beast called "Karkadan" will carry off a great elephant on its horn and graze about the island and the sea-coast therewith and take no heed of it, till the elephant dieth and its fat, melting in the sun, runneth down into the rhinoceros's eyes and blindeth him, so that he lieth down on the shore. Then comes the bird Rukh and carrieth off both the rhinoceros's eyes and blindeth him, so that he lieth down on the shore. Then comes the bird Rukh and carrieth off both the rhinoceros and that which is on its horn to feed its young withal. Moreover, I saw in this island many kinds of oxen and buffalos, whose like are not found in our country. Here I sold some of the diamonds which I had by me for gold dinars and silver dirhams and bartered others for the produce of the country; and, loading them upon beasts of burden, fared on with the merchants from valley to valley and town to town, buying and selling and viewing foreign countries and the works and creatures of Allah, till we came to Bassorah-city, where we abode a few days, after which I continued my journey to Baghdad.—And Shahrazad perceived the dawn of day and ceased to say her permitted say.

When it was the Five Hundred and Forty-sixth Night,

She said, It hath reached me, O auspicious King, that when Sindbad the Seaman returned from his travel to Baghdad, the House of Peace, he arrived at home with great store of diamonds and money and goods. (Continued he) I foregathered with my friends and relations and gave alms and largesse and bestowed curious gifts and made presents to all my friends and companions. Then I betook myself to eating well and drinking well and wearing fine clothes and making merry with my fellows, and forgot all my sufferings in the pleasures of return to the solace and delight of life, with light heart and broadened breast. And every one who heard of my return came and questioned me of my adventures and of foreign countries, and I related to them all that had befallen me, and the much I had suffered, whereat they wondered and gave me joy of my safe return. "This, then is the end of the story of my second voyage; and to-morrow, Inshallah! I will tell you what befel me in my third voyage." The company marvelled at his story and supped with him; after which he ordered an hundred dinars of gold to be given to the Porter, who took the sum with many thanks and blessings (which he stinted not even when he reached home) and went his way, wondering at what he had heard. Next morning as soon as day came in its sheen and shone, he rose and praying the dawn-prayer, repaired to the house of Sindbad the Seaman, even as he had bidden him, and went in and gave him good-morrow. The merchant welcomed him and made him sit with him, till the rest of the company arrived; and when they had well eaten and drunken and were merry with joy and jollity, their host began by saying, "Hearken, O my brothers, to what I am about to tell you; for it is even more wondrous than what you have already heard; but Allah alone kenneth what things His Omniscience concealed from man! And listen to

THE THIRD VOYAGE OF SINDBAD THE SEAMAN.

As I told you yesterday, I returned from my second voyage overjoyed at my safety and with great increase of wealth, Allah having requited me all that I had wasted and lost, and I abode awhile in Baghdad-city savouring the utmost ease and prosperity and comfort and happiness, till the carnal man was once more seized with longing for travel and diversion and adventure, and yearned after traffic and lucre and emolument, for that the human heart is naturally prone to evil. So making up my mind I laid in great plenty of goods suitable for a sea-voyage and repairing to Bassorah, went down to the shore and found there a fine ship ready to sail, with a full crew and a numerous company of merchants, men of worth and substance; faith, piety and consideration. I embarked with them and we set sail on the blessing of Allah Almighty and on His aidance and His favour to bring our voyage to a safe and prosperous issue and already we congratulated one another on our good fortune and boon voyage. We fared on from sea to sea and from island to island and city to city, in all delight and contentment, buying and selling wherever we touched, and taking our solace and our pleasure, till one day when, as we sailed athwart the dashing sea, swollen with clashing billows, behold, the master (who stood on the gunwale examining the ocean in all directions) cried out with a great cry, and buffeted his face and pluckt out his beard and rent his raiment, and bade furl the sail and cast the anchors. So we said to him, "O Rais, what is the matter?" "Know, O my brethren (Allah preserve you!), that the wind hath gotten the better of us and hath driven us out of our course into mid-ocean, and destiny, for our ill luck, hath brought us to the Mountain of the Zughb, a hairy folk like apes, [26] among whom no man ever fell and came forth alive; and my heart presageth that we all be dead men." Hardly had the master made an end of his speech when the apes were upon us. They surrounded the ship on all sides swarming like locusts and crowding the shore. They were the most frightful of wild creatures, covered with black hair like felt, foul of favour and small of stature, being but four spans high, yellow-eyed and black-faced; none knoweth their language nor what they are, and they shun the company of men. We feared to slay them or strike them or drive them away, because of their inconceivable multitude; lest, if we hurt one, the rest fall on us and slay us, for numbers prevail over courage; so we let them do their will, albeit we feared they would plunder our goods and gear. They swarmed up the cables and gnawed them asunder, and on like wise they did with all the ropes of the ship, so that it fell off from the wind and stranded upon their mountainous coast. Then they laid hands on all the merchants and crew, and landing us on the island, made off with the ship and its cargo and went their ways, we wot not whither. We were thus left on the island, eating of its fruits and pot-herbs and drinking of its streams till, one day, we espied in its midst what seemed an inhabited house. So we made for it as fast as our feet could carry us and behold, it was a castle strong and tall, compassed about with a lofty wall, and having a two-leaved gate of ebony-wood both of which leaves open stood. We entered and found within a space wide and bare like a great square, round which stood many high doors open thrown, and at the farther end a long bench of stone and brasiers, with cooking gear hanging thereon and about it great plenty of bones; but we saw no one and marvelled thereat with exceeding wonder. Then we sat down in the courtyard a little while and presently falling asleep, slept from the forenoon till sundown, when lo! the earth trembled under our feet and the air rumbled with a terrible tone. Then there came down upon us, from the top of the castle, a huge creature in the likeness of a man, black of colour, tall and big of bulk, as he were a great date-tree, with eyes like coals of fire and eye-teeth like boar's tusks and a vast big gape like the mouth of a well. Moreover, he had long loose lips like camel's, hanging down upon his breast and ears like two Jarms [27] falling over his shoulder-blades and the nails of his hands were like the claws of a lion. [28] When we saw this frightful giant, we were like to faint and every moment increased our fear and terror; and we became as dead men for excess of horror and affright.—And Shahrazad perceived the dawn of day and ceased saying her permitted say.

When it was the Five Hundred and Forty-seventh Night,

She said, It hath reached me, O auspicious King, that Sindbad the Seaman continued:—When we saw this frightful giant we were struck with exceeding terror and horror. And after trampling upon the earth, he sat awhile on the bench; then he arose and coming to us seized me by the arm choosing me out from among my comrades the merchants. He took me up in his hand and turning me over felt me, as a butcher feeleth a sheep he is about to slaughter, and I but a little mouthful in his hands; but finding me lean and fleshless for stress of toil and trouble and weariness, let me go and took up another, whom in like manner he turned over and felt and let go; nor did he cease to feel and turn over the rest of us, one after another, till he came to the master of the ship. Now he was a sturdy, stout, broad-shouldered wight, fat and in full vigour; so he pleased the giant, who seized him, as a butcher seizeth a beast, and throwing him down, set his foot on his neck and brake it; after which he fetched a long spit and thrusting it up his backside, brought it forth of the crown of his head. Then, lighting a fierce fire, he set over it the spit with the Rais thereon, and turned it over the coals, till the flesh was roasted, when he took the spit off the fire and set it like a Kabáb-stick before him. Then he tare the body, limb from limb, as one jointeth a chicken and, rending the flesh with his nails, fell to eating of it and gnawing the bones, till there was nothing left but some of these, which he threw on one side of the wall. This done, he sat for a while; then he lay down on the stone-bench and fell asleep, snarking and snoring like the gurgling of a lamb or a cow with its throat cut; nor did he awake till morning, when he rose and fared forth and went his ways. As soon as we were certified that he was gone, we began to talk with one another, weeping and bemoaning ourselves for the risk we ran, and saying, "Would Heaven we had been drowned in the sea or that the apes had eaten us! That were better than to be roasted over the coals; by Allah, this is a vile, foul death! But whatso the Lord willeth must come to pass and there is no Majesty and there is no Might, save in Him, the Glorious, the Great! We shall assuredly perish miserably and none will know of us; as there is no escape for us from this place." Then we arose and roamed about the island, hoping that haply we might find a place to hide us in or a means of flight, for indeed death was a light matter to us, provided we were not roasted over the fire [29] and eaten. However, we could find no hiding-place and the evening overtook us; so, of the excess of our terror, we returned to the castle and sat down awhile. Presently, the earth trembled under our feet and the black ogre came up to us and turning us over, felt one after other, till he found a man to his liking, whom he took and served as he had done the captain, killing and roasting and eating him: after which he lay down on the bench [30] and slept all night, snarking and snoring like a beast with its throat cut, till daybreak, when he arose and went out as before. Then we drew together and conversed and said one to other, "By Allah, we had better throw ourselves into the sea and be drowned than die roasted; for this is an abominable death!" Quoth one of us, "Hear ye my words! let us cast about to kill him, and be at peace from the grief of him and rid the Moslems of his barbarity and tyranny." Then said I, "Hear me, O my brothers; if there is nothing for it but to slay him, let us carry some of this firewood and planks down to the sea-shore and make us a boat wherein, if we succeed in slaughtering him, we may either embark and let the waters carry us whither Allah willeth, or else abide here till some ship pass, when we will take passage in it. If we fail to kill him, we will embark in the boat and put out to sea; and if we be drowned, we shall at least escape being roasted over a kitchen fire with sliced weasands; whilst, if we escape, we escape, and if we be drowned, we die martyrs." "By Allah," said they all, "this rede is a right;" and we agreed upon this, and set about carrying it out. So we haled down to the beach the pieces of wood which lay about the bench; and, making a boat, moored it to the strand, after which we stowed therein somewhat of victual and returned to the castle. As soon as evening fell the earth trembled under our feet and in came the blackamoor upon us, snarling like a dog about to bite. He came up to us and feeling us and turning us over one by one, took one of us and did with him as he had done before and ate him, after which he lay down on the bench and snored and snorted like thunder. As soon as we were assured that he slept, we arose and taking two iron spits of those standing there, heated them in the fiercest of the fire, till they were red-hot, like burning coals, when we gripped fast hold of them and going up to the giant, as he lay snoring on the bench, thrust them into his eyes and pressed upon them, all of us, with our united might, so that his eyeballs burst and he became stone blind. Thereupon he cried with a great cry, whereat our hearts trembled, and springing up from the bench, he fell a-groping after us, blind-fold. We fled from him right and left and he saw us not, for his sight was altogether blent; but we were in terrible fear of him and made sure we were dead men despairing of escape. Then he found the door, feeling for it with his hands and went out roaring aloud; and behold, the earth shook under us, for the noise of his roaring, and we quaked for fear. As he quitted the castle we followed him and betook ourselves to the place where we had moored our boat, saying to one another, "If this accursed abide absent till the going down of the sun and come not to the castle, we shall know that he is dead; and if he come back, we will embark in the boat and paddle till we escape, committing our affair to Allah." But, as we spoke, behold, up came the blackamoor with other two as they were Ghuls, fouler and more frightful than he, with eyes like red-hot coals; which when we saw, we hurried into the boat and casting off the moorings paddled away and pushed out to sea. [31] As soon as the ogres caught sight of us, they cried out at us and running down to the sea-shore, fell a-pelting us with rocks, whereof some fell amongst us and others fell into the sea. We paddled with all our might till we were beyond their reach, but the most part of us were slain by the rock-throwing, and the winds and waves sported with us and carried us into the midst of the dashing sea, swollen with billows clashing. We knew not whither we went and my fellows died one after another, till there remained but three, myself and two others;—And Shahrazad perceived the dawn of day and ceased to say her permitted say.

When it was the Five Hundred and Forty-eighth Night,

She said, It hath reached me, O auspicious King, that Sindbad the Seaman thus continued:—Most part of us were slain by the rock-throwing and only three of us remained on board the boat for, as often as one died, we threw him into the sea. We were sore exhausted for stress of hunger, but we took courage and heartened one another and worked for dear life and paddled with main and might, till the winds cast us upon an island, as we were dead men for fatigue and fear and famine. We landed on the island and walked about it for a while, finding that it abounded in trees and streams and birds; and we ate of the fruits and rejoiced in our escape from the black and our deliverance from the perils of the sea; and thus we did till nightfall, when we lay down and fell asleep for excess of fatigue. But we had hardly closed our eyes before we were aroused by a hissing sound like the sough of wind, and awaking, saw a serpent like a dragon, a seld-seen sight, of monstrous make and belly of enormous bulk which lay in a circle around us. Presently it reared its head and, seizing one of my companions, swallowed him up to his shoulders; then it gulped down the rest of him, and we heard his ribs crack in its belly. Presently it went its way, and we abode in sore amazement and grief for our comrade and mortal fear for ourselves, saying, "By Allah, this is a marvellous thing! Each kind of death that threatened us is more terrible than the last. We were rejoicing in our escape from the black ogre and our deliverance from the perils of the sea; but now we have fallen into that which is worse. There is no Majesty and there is no Might save in Allah! By the Almighty, we have escaped from the blackamoor and from drowning: but how shall we escape from this abominable and viperish monster?" Then we walked about the island, eating of its fruits and drinking of its streams till dusk, when we climbed up into a high tree and went to sleep there, I being on the topmost bough. As soon as it was dark night, up came the serpent, looking right and left; and, making for the tree whereon we were, climbed up to my comrade and swallowed him down to his shoulders. Then it coiled about the bole [32] with him, whilst I, who could not take my eyes off the sight, heard his bones crack in its belly, and it swallowed him whole, after which it slid down from the tree. When the day broke and the light showed me that the serpent was gone, I came down, as I were a dead man for stress of fear and anguish, and thought to cast myself into the sea and be at rest from the woes of the world; but could not bring myself to this, for verily life is dear. So I took five pieces of wood, broad and long, and bound one crosswise to the soles of my feet and others in like fashion on my right and left sides and over my breast; and the broadest and largest I bound across my head and made them fast with ropes. Then I lay down on the ground on my back, so that I was completely fenced in by the pieces of wood, which enclosed me like a bier. [33] So as soon as it was dark, up came the serpent, as usual, and made towards me, but could not get at me to swallow me for the wood that fenced me in. So it wriggled round me on every side, whilst I looked on, like one dead by reason of my terror; and every now and then it would glide away and come back; but as often as it tried to come at me, it was hindered by the pieces of wood wherewith I had bound myself on every side. It ceased not to beset me thus from sundown till dawn, but when the light of day shone upon the beast it made off, in the utmost fury and extreme disappointment. Then I put out my hand and unbound myself, well-nigh down among the dead men for fear and suffering; and went down to the island-shore, whence a ship afar off in the midst of the waves suddenly struck my sight. So I tore off a great branch of a tree and made signs with it to the crew, shouting out the while; which when the ship's company saw they said to another, "We must stand in and see what this is; peradventure 'tis a man." So they made for the island and presently heard my cries, whereupon they took me on board and questioned me of my case. I told them all my adventures from first to last, whereat they marvelled mightily and covered my shame [34] with some of their clothes. Moreover, they set before me somewhat of food and I ate my fill and I drank cold sweet water and was mightily refreshed; and Allah Almighty quickened me after I was virtually dead. So I praised the Most Highest and thanked Him for His favours and exceeding mercies, and my heart revived in me after utter despair, till meseemed as if all I had suffered were but a dream I had dreamed. We sailed on with a fair wind the Almighty sent us till we came to an island, called Al-Saláhitah, [35] which aboundeth in sandal-wood when the captain cast anchor,—And Shahrazad perceived the dawn of day and ceased saying her permitted say.

When it was the Five Hundred and Forty-ninth Night,

She said, It hath reached me, O auspicious King, that Sindbad the Seaman continued:—And when we had cast anchor, the merchants and the sailors landed with their goods to sell and to buy. Then the captain turned to me and said, "Hark'ee, thou art a stranger and a pauper and tellest us that thou hast undergone frightful hardship; wherefore I have a mind to benefit thee with somewhat that may further thee to thy native land, so thou wilt ever bless me and pray for me." "So be it," answered I; "thou shalt have my prayers." Quoth he, "Know then that there was with us a man, a traveller, whom we lost, and we know not if he be alive or dead, for we had no news of him; so I purpose to commit his bales of goods to thy charge, that thou mayst sell them in this island. A part of the proceeds we will give thee as an equivalent for thy pains and service, and the rest we will keep till we return to Baghdad, where we will enquire for his family and deliver it to them, together with the unsold goods. Say me then, wilt thou undertake the charge and land and sell them as other merchants do?" I replied "Hearkening and obedience to thee, O my lord; and great is thy kindness to me," and thanked him; whereupon he bade the sailors and porters bear the bales in question ashore and commit them to my charge. The ship's scribe asked him, "O master, what bales are these and what merchant's name shall I write upon them?"; and he answered, "Write on them the name of Sindbad the Seaman, him who was with us in the ship and whom we lost at the Rukh's island, and of whom we have no tidings; for we mean this stranger to sell them; and we will give him a part of the price for his pains and keep the rest till we return to Baghdad where, if we find the owner we will make it over to him, and if not, to his family." And the clerk said, "Thy words are apposite and thy rede is right." Now when I heard the captain give orders for the bales to be inscribed with my name, I said to myself, "By Allah, I am Sindbad the Seaman!" So I armed myself with courage and patience and waited till all the merchants had landed and were gathered together, talking and chaffering about buying and selling; then I went up to the captain and asked him, "O my lord, knowest thou what manner of man was this Sindbad, whose goods thou hast committed to me for sale?"; and he answered, "I know of him naught save that he was a man from Baghdad-city, Sindbad hight the Seaman, who was drowned with many others when we lay anchored at such an island and I have heard nothing of him since then." At this I cried out with a great cry and said, "O captain, whom Allah keep! know that I am that Sindbad the Seaman and that I was not drowned, but when thou castest anchor at the island, I landed with the rest of the merchants and crew; and I sat down in a pleasant place by myself and ate somewhat of food I had with me and enjoyed myself till I became drowsy and was drowned in sleep; and when I awoke, I found no ship and none near me. These goods are my goods and these bales are my bales; and all the merchants who fetch jewels from the Valley of Diamonds saw me there and will bear me witness that I am the very Sindbad the Seaman; for I related to them everything that had befallen me and told them how you forgot me and left me sleeping on the island, and that betided me which betided me." When the passengers and crew heard my words, they gathered about me and some of them believed me and others disbelieved; but presently, behold, one of the merchants, hearing me mention the Valley of Diamonds, came up to me and said to them, "Hear what I say, good people! When I related to you the most wonderful thing in my travels, and I told you that, at the time we cast down our slaughtered animals into the Valley of Serpents (I casting with the rest as was my wont), there came up a man hanging to mine, ye believed me not and gave me the lie." "Yes," quoth they, "thou didst tell us some such tale, but we had no call to credit thee." He resumed, "Now this is the very man, by token that he gave me diamonds of great value, and high price whose like are not to be found, requiting me more than would have come up sticking to my quarter of meat; and I companied with him to Bassorah-city, where he took leave of us and went on to his native stead, whilst we returned to our own land. This is he; and he told us his name, Sindbad the Seaman, and how the ship left him on the desert island. And know ye that Allah hath sent him hither, so might the truth of my story be made manifest to you. Moreover, these are his goods for, when he first foregathered with us, he told us of them; and the truth of his words is patent." Hearing the merchant's speech the captain came up to me and considered me straitly awhile, after which he said, "What was the mark on thy bales?" "Thus and thus," answered I, and reminded him of somewhat that had passed between him and me, when I shipped with him from Bassorah. Thereupon he was convinced that I was indeed

Sindbad the Seaman and took me round the neck and gave me joy of my safety, saying, "By Allah, O my lord, thy case is indeed wondrous and thy tale marvellous; but lauded be Allah who hath brought thee and me together again, and who hath restored to thee thy goods and gear!"—And Shahrazad perceived the dawn of day and ceased to say her permitted say.

When it was the Five Hundred and Fiftieth Night,

She said, It hath reached me, O auspicious King, that Sindbad the Seaman thus continued:—"Alhamdolillah!" quoth the captain, "lauded be Allah who hath restored unto thee thy goods and gear." Then I disposed of my merchandise to the best of my skill, and profited largely on them whereat I rejoiced with exceeding joy and congratulated myself on my safety and the recovery of my goods. We ceased not to buy and sell at the several islands till we came to the land of Hind, where we bought cloves and ginger and all manner spices; and thence we fared on to the land of Sind, where also we bought and sold. In these Indian seas, I saw wonders without number or count, amongst others a fish like a cow which bringeth forth its young and suckleth them like human beings; and of its skin bucklers are made. [36] There were eke fishes like asses and camels [37] and tortoises twenty cubits wide. [38] And I saw also a bird that cometh out of a sea-shell and layeth eggs and hatcheth her chicks on the surface of the water, never coming up from the sea to the land. [39] Then we set sail again with a fair wind and the blessing of Almighty Allah; and, after a prosperous voyage, arrived safe and sound at Bassorah. Here I abode a few days and presently returned to Baghdad where I went at once to my quarter and my house and saluted my family and familiars and friends. I had gained on this voyage what was beyond count and reckoning, so I gave alms and largesse and clad the widow and the orphan, by way of thanksgiving for my happy return, and fell to feasting and making merry with my companions and intimates and forgot, while eating well and drinking well and dressing well, everything that had befallen me and all the perils and hardships I had suffered. "These, then, are the most admirable things I sighted on my third voyage, and to-morrow, an it be the will of Allah, you shall come to me and I will relate the adventures of my fourth voyage, which is still more wonderful than those you have already heard." (Saith he who telleth the tale), Then Sindbad the Seaman bade give Sindbad the Landsman an hundred golden dinars as of wont and called for food. So they spread the tables and the company ate the night-meal and went their ways, marvelling at the tale they had heard. The Porter after taking his gold passed the night in his own house, also wondering at what his namesake the Seaman had told him, and as soon as day broke and the morning showed with its sheen and shone, he rose and praying the dawn-prayer betook himself to Sindbad the Seaman, who returned his salute and received him with an open breast and cheerful favour and made him sit with him till the rest of the company arrived, when he caused set on food and they ate and drank and made merry. Then Sindbad the Seaman bespake them and related to them the narrative of

THE FOURTH VOYAGE OF SINDBAD THE SEAMAN.

Know, O my brethren that after my return from my third voyage and foregathering with my friends, and forgetting all my perils and hardships in the enjoyment of ease and comfort and repose, I was visited one day by a company of merchants who sat down with me and talked of foreign travel and traffic, till the old bad man within me yearned to go with them and enjoy the sight of strange countries, and I longed for the society of the various races of mankind and for traffic and profit. So I resolved to travel with them and buying the necessaries for a long voyage, and great store of costly goods, more than ever before, transported them from Baghdad to Bassorah where I took ship with the merchants in question, who were of the chief of the town. We set out, trusting in the blessing of Almighty Allah; and with a favouring breeze and the best conditions we sailed from island to island and sea to sea, till, one day, there arose against us a contrary wind and the captain cast out his anchors and brought the ship to a standstill, fearing lest she should founder in mid-ocean. Then we all fell to prayer and humbling ourselves before the Most High; but, as we were thus engaged there smote us a furious squall which tore the sails to rags and tatters: the anchor-cable parted and, the ship foundering, we were cast into the sea, goods and all. I kept myself afloat by swimming half the day, till, when I had given myself up for lost, the Almighty threw in my way one of the planks of the ship, whereon I and some others of the merchants scrambled.—And Shahrazad perceived the dawn of day and ceased saying her permitted say.

When it was the Five Hundred and Fifty-first Night,

She said, It hath reached me, O auspicious King, that Sindbad the Seaman continued as follows:—And when the ship foundered I scrambled on to a plank with some others of the merchants and, mounting it as we would a horse, paddled with our feet in the sea. We abode thus a day and a night, the wind and waves helping us on, and on the second day shortly before the mid-time between sunrise and noon [40] the breeze freshened and the sea wrought and the rising waves cast us upon an island, well-nigh dead bodies for weariness and want of sleep, cold and hunger and fear and thirst. We walked about the shore and found abundance of herbs, whereof we ate enough to keep breath in body and to stay our failing spirits, then lay down and slept till morning hard by the sea. And when morning came with its sheen and shone, we arose and walked about the island to the right and left, till we came in sight of an inhabited house afar off. So we made towards it, and ceased not walking till we reached the door thereof when lo! a number of naked men issued from it and without saluting us or a word said, laid hold of us masterfully and carried us to their king, who signed us to sit. So we sat down and they set food before us such as we knew not [41] and whose like we had never seen in all our lives. My companions ate of it, for stress of hunger, but my stomach revolted from it and I would not eat; and my refraining from it was, by Allah's favour, the cause of my being alive till now: for no sooner had my comrades tasted of it than their reason fled and their condition changed and they began to devour it like madmen possessed of an evil spirit. Then the savages gave them to drink of cocoa-nut oil and anointed them therewith; and straightway after drinking thereof, their eyes turned into their heads and they fell to eating greedily, against their wont. When I saw this, I was confounded and concerned for them, nor was I less anxious about myself, for fear of the naked folk. So I watched them narrowly, and it was not long before I discovered them to be a tribe of Magian cannibals whose King was a Ghul. [42] All who came to their country or whoso they caught in their valleys or on their roads they brought to this King and fed them upon that food and anointed them with that oil, whereupon their stomachs dilated that they might eat largely, whilst their reason fled and they lost the power of thought and became idiots. Then they stuffed them with cocoa-nut oil and the aforesaid food, till they became fat and gross, when they slaughtered them by cutting their throats and roasted them for the King's eating; but, as for the savages themselves, they ate human flesh raw. [43] When I saw this, I was sore dismayed for myself and my comrades, who were now become so stupefied that they knew not what was done with them and the naked folk committed them to one who used every day to lead them out and pasture them on the island like cattle. And they wandered amongst the trees and rested at will, thus waxing very fat. As for me, I wasted away and became sickly for fear and hunger and my flesh shrivelled on my bones; which when the savages saw, they left me alone and took no thought of me and so far forgot me that one day I gave them the slip and walking out of their place made for the beach which was distant and there espied a very old man seated on a high place, girt by the waters. I looked at him and knew him for the herdsman, who had charge of pasturing my fellows, and with him were many others in like case. As soon as he saw me, he knew me to be in possession of my reason and not afflicted like the rest whom he was pasturing; so signed to me from afar, as who should say, "Turn back and take the right-hand road, for that will lead thee into the King's highway." So I turned back, as he bade me, and followed the right-hand road, now running for fear and then walking leisurely to rest me, till I was out of the old man's sight. By this time, the sun had gone down and the darkness set in; so I sat down to rest and would have slept, but sleep came not to me that night, for stress of fear and famine and fatigue. When the night was half spent, I rose and walked on, till the day broke in all its beauty and the sun rose over the heads of the lofty hills and athwart the low gravelly plains. Now I was weary and hungry and thirsty; so I ate my fill of herbs and grasses that grew in the island and kept life in body and stayed my stomach, after which I set out again and fared on all that day and the next night, staying my greed with roots and herbs; nor did I cease walking for seven days and their nights, till the morn of the eighth day, when I caught sight of a faint object in the distance. So I made towards it, though my heart quaked for all I had suffered first and last, and behold it was a company of men gathering pepper-grains. [44] As soon as they saw me, they hastened up to me and surrounding me on all sides, said to me, "Who art thou and whence come?" I replied, "Know, O folk, that I am a poor stranger," and acquainted them with my case and all the hardships and perils I had suffered,—And Shahrazad perceived the dawn of day and ceased to say her permitted say.

When it was the Five Hundred and Fifty-second Night,

She said, It hath reached me, O auspicious King, that Sindbad the Seaman continued:—And the men gathering pepper in the island questioned me of my case, when I acquainted them with all the hardships and perils I had suffered and how I had fled from the savages; whereat they marvelled and gave me joy of my safety, saying, "By Allah, this is wonderful! But how didst thou escape from these blacks who swarm in the island and devour all who fall in with them; nor is any safe from them, nor can any get out of their clutches?" And after I had told them the fate of my companions, they made me sit by them, till they got quit of their work; and fetched me somewhat of good food, which I ate, for I was hungry, and rested awhile, after which they took ship with me and carrying me to their island-home brought me before their King, who returned my salute and received me honourably and questioned me of my case. I told him all that had befallen me, from the day of my leaving Baghdad-city, whereupon he wondered with great wonder at my adventures, he and his courtiers, and bade me sit by him; then he called for food and I ate with him what sufficed me and washed my hands and returned thanks to Almighty Allah for all His favours praising Him and glorifying Him. Then I left the King and walked for solace about the city, which I found wealthy and populous, abounding in market-streets well stocked with food and merchandise and full of buyers and sellers. So I rejoiced at having reached so pleasant a place and took my ease there after my fatigues; and I made friends with the townsfolk, nor was it long before I became more in honour and favour with them and their King than any of the chief men of the realm. Now I saw that all the citizens, great and small, rode fine horses, high-priced and thorough-bred, without saddles or housings, whereat I wondered and said to the King, "Wherefore, O my lord, dost thou not ride with a saddle? Therein is ease for the rider and increase of power." "What is a saddle?" asked he: "I never saw nor used such a thing in all my life;" and I answered, "With thy permission I will make thee a saddle, that thou mayest ride on it and see the comfort thereof." And quoth he, "Do so." So quoth I to him, "Furnish me with some wood," which being brought, I sought me a clever carpenter and sitting by him showed him how to make the saddle-tree, portraying for him the fashion thereof in ink on the wood. Then I took wool and teased it and made felt of it, and, covering the saddle-tree with leather, stuffed it and polished it and attached the girth and stirrup leathers; after which I fetched a blacksmith and described to him the fashion of the stirrups and bridle-bit. So he forged a fine pair of stirrups and a bit, and filed them smooth and tinned [45] them. Moreover, I made fast to them fringes of silk and fitted bridle-leathers to the bit. Then I fetched one of the best of the royal horses and saddling and bridling him, hung the stirrups to the saddle and led him to the King. The thing took his fancy and he thanked me; then he mounted and rejoiced greatly in the saddle and rewarded me handsomely for my work. When the King's Wazir saw the saddle, he asked of me one like it and I made it for him. Furthermore, all the grandees and officers of state came for saddles to me; so I fell to making saddles (having taught the craft to the carpenter and blacksmith), and selling them to all who sought, till I amassed great wealth and became in high honour and great favour with the King and his household and grandees. I abode thus till, one day, as I was sitting with the King in all respect and contentment, he said to me, "Know thou, O such an one, thou art become one of us, dear as a brother, and we hold thee in such regard and affection that we cannot part with thee nor suffer thee to leave our city; wherefore I desire of thee obedience in a certain matter, and I will not have thee gainsay me." Answered I, "O King, what is it thou desirest of me? Far be it from me to gainsay thee in aught, for I am indebted to thee for many favours and bounties and much kindness, and (praised be Allah!) I am become one of thy servants." Quoth he, "I have a mind to marry thee to a fair, clever and agreeable wife who is wealthy as she is beautiful; so thou mayst be naturalised and domiciled with us: I will lodge thee with me in my palace; wherefore oppose me not neither cross me in this." When I heard these words I was ashamed and held my peace nor could make him any answer, [46] by reason of my much bashfulness before him. Asked he, "Why dost thou not reply to me, O my son?"; and I answered saying, "O my master, it is thine to command, O King of the age!" So he summoned the Kazi and the witnesses and married me straightway to a lady of a noble tree and high pedigree; wealthy in moneys and means; the flower of an ancient race; of surpassing beauty and grace, and the owner of farms and estates and many a dwelling-place.—And Shahrazad perceived the dawn of day and ceased saying her permitted say.

When it was the Five Hundred and Fifty-third Night,

She said, It hath reached me, O auspicious King, that Sindbad the Seaman continued in these words:—Now after the King my master had married me to this choice wife, he also gave me a great and goodly house standing alone, together with slaves and officers, and assigned me pay and allowances. So I became in all ease and contentment and delight and forgot everything which had befallen me of weariness and trouble and hardship; for I loved my wife with fondest love and she loved me no less, and we were as one and abode in the utmost comfort of life and in its happiness. And I said in myself, "When I return to my native land, I will carry her with me." But whatso is predestined to a man, that needs must be, and none knoweth what shall befal him. We lived thus a great while, till Almighty Allah bereft one of my neighbours of his wife. Now he was a gossip of mine; so hearing the cry of the keeners I went in to condole with him on his loss and found him in very ill plight, full of trouble and weary of soul and mind. I

condoled with him and comforted him, saying, "Mourn not for thy wife
who hath now found the mercy of Allah; the Lord will surely give thee
a better in her stead and thy name shall be great and thy life shall be
long in the land, Inshallah!" [47] But he wept bitter tears and replied,
"O my friend, how can I marry another wife and how shall Allah
replace her to me with a better than she, whenas I have but one day left
to live?" "O my brother," said I, "return to thy senses and announce not
the glad tidings of thine own death, for thou art well, sound and in good
case." "By thy life, O my friend," rejoined he, "to-morrow thou wilt
lose me and wilt never see me again till the Day of Resurrection." I
asked, "How so?" and he answered, "This very day they bury my wife,
and they bury me with her in one tomb; for it is the custom with us, if
the wife die first, to bury the husband alive with her and in like manner
the wife, if the husband die first; so that neither may enjoy life after
losing his or her mate." "By Allah," cried I, "this is a most vile, lewd
custom and not to be endured of any!" Meanwhile, behold, the most
part of the townsfolk came in and fell to condoling with my gossip for
his wife and for himself. Presently they laid the dead woman out, as
was their wont; and, setting her on a bier, carried her and her husband
without the city, till they came to a place in the side of the mountain at
the end of the island by the sea; and here they raised a great rock and
discovered the mouth of a stone-rivetted pit or well, [48] leading down
into a vast underground cavern that ran beneath the mountain. Into this
pit they threw the corpse, then tying a rope of palm-fibres under the
husband's armpits, they let him down into the cavern, and with him a
great pitcher of fresh water and seven scones by was of viaticum. [49]
When he came to the bottom, he loosed himself from the rope and they
drew it up; and, stopping the mouth of the pit with the great stone, they
returned to the city, leaving my friend in the cavern with his dead wife.
When I saw this, I said to myself, "By Allah, this fashion of death is
more grievous than the first!" And I went in to the King and said to
him, "O my lord, why do ye bury the quick with the dead?" Quoth he,
"It hath been the custom, thou must know, of our forbears and our
olden Kings from time immemorial, if the husband die first, to bury his
wife with him, and the like with the wife, so we may not sever them,
alive or dead." I asked, "O King of the age, if the wife of a foreigner
like myself die among you, deal ye with him as with yonder man?"; and
he answered, "Assuredly, we do with him even as thou hast seen."
When I heard this, my gall-bladder was like to burst, for the violence of
my dismay and concern for myself: my wit became dazed; I felt as if in
a vile dungeon; and hated their society; for I went about in fear lest my
wife should die before me and they bury me alive with her. However,

after a while, I comforted myself, saying, "Haply I shall predecease her, or shall have returned to my own land before she die, for none knoweth which shall go first and which shall go last." Then I applied myself to diverting my mind from this thought with various occupations; but it was not long before my wife sickened and complained and took to her pillow and fared after a few days to the mercy of Allah; and the King and the rest of the folk came, as was their wont, to condole with me and her family and to console us for her loss and not less to condole with me for myself. Then the women washed her and arraying her in her richest raiment and golden ornaments, necklaces and jewellery, laid her on the bier and bore her to the mountain aforesaid, where they lifted the cover of the pit and cast her in; after which all my intimates and acquaintances and my wife's kith and kin came round me, to farewell me in my lifetime and console me for my own death, whilst I cried out among them, saying, "Almighty Allah never made it lawful to bury the quick with the dead! I am a stranger, not one of your kind; and I cannot abear your custom, and had I known it I never would have wedded among you!" They heard me not and paid no heed to my words, but laying hold of me, bound me by force and let me down into the cavern, with a large gugglet of sweet water and seven cakes of bread, according to their custom. When I came to the bottom, they called out to me to cast myself loose from the cords, but I refused to do so; so they threw them down on me and, closing the mouth of the pit with the stones aforesaid, went their ways,—And Shahrazad perceived the dawn of day and ceased to say her permitted say.

When it was the Five Hundred and Fifty-fourth Night,

She said, It hath reached me, O auspicious King, that Sindbad the Seaman continued:—When they left me in the cavern with my dead wife and, closing the mouth of the pit, went their ways, I looked about me and found myself in a vast cave full of dead bodies, that exhaled a fulsome and loathsome smell and the air was heavy with the groans of the dying. Thereupon I fell to blaming myself for what I had done, saying, "By Allah, I deserve all that hath befallen me and all that shall befal me! What curse was upon me to take a wife in this city? There is no Majesty and there is no Might save in Allah, the Glorious, the Great! As often as I say, I have escaped from one calamity, I fall into a worse. By Allah, this is an abominable death to die! Would Heaven I had died a decent death and been washed and shrouded like a man and a Moslem. Would I had been drowned at sea or perished in the mountains! It were better than to die this miserable death!" And on such wise I kept blaming my own folly and greed of gain in that black hole, knowing not night from day; and I ceased not to ban the Foul Fiend and to bless the Almighty Friend. Then I threw myself down on the bones of the dead and lay there, imploring Allah's help and in the violence of my despair, invoking death which came not to me, till the fire of hunger burned my stomach and thirst set my throat aflame when I sat up and feeling for the bread, ate a morsel and upon it swallowed a mouthful of water. After this, the worst night I ever knew, I arose, and exploring the cavern, found that it extended a long way with hollows in its sides; and its floor was strewn with dead bodies and rotten bones, that had lain there from olden time. So I made myself a place in a cavity of the cavern, afar from the corpses lately thrown down and there slept. I abode thus a long while, till my provision was like to give out; and yet I ate not save once every day or second day; nor did I drink more than an occasional draught, for fear my victual should fail me before my death; and I said to myself, "Eat little and drink little; belike the Lord shall vouchsafe deliverance to thee!" One day, as I sat thus, pondering my case and bethinking me how I should do, when my bread and water should be exhausted, behold, the stone that covered the opening was suddenly rolled away and the light streamed down upon me. Quoth I, "I wonder what is the matter: haply they have brought another corpse." Then I espied folk standing about the mouth of the pit, who presently let down a dead man and a live woman, weeping and bemoaning herself, and with her an ampler supply of bread and water than usual. [50] I saw her and she was a beautiful woman; but she saw me not; and they closed up the opening and went away. Then I took the leg-bone of a dead man and, going up to the woman, smote her on the crown of the head; and she cried one cry and fell down in a swoon. I smote her a second and a third time, till she was dead, when I laid hands on her bread and water and found on her great plenty of ornaments and rich apparel, necklaces, jewels and gold trinkets; [51] for it was their custom to bury women in all their finery. I carried the vivers to my sleeping place in the cavern-side and ate and drank of them sparingly, no more than sufficed to keep the life in me, lest the provaunt come speedily to an end and I perish of hunger and thirst. Yet did I never wholly lose hope in Almighty Allah. I abode thus a great while, killing all the live folk they let down into the cavern and taking their provisions of meat and drink; till one day, as I slept, I was awakened by something scratching and burrowing among the bodies in a corner of the cave and said, "What can this be?" fearing wolves or hyenas. So I sprang up and seizing the leg-bone aforesaid, made for the noise. As soon as the thing was ware of me, it fled from me into the inward of the cavern, and lo! it was a wild beast. However, I followed it to the further end, till I saw afar off a point of light not bigger than a star, now appearing and then disappearing. So I made for it, and as I drew near, it grew larger and brighter, till I was certified that it was a crevice in the rock, leading to the open country; and I said to myself, "There must be some reason for this opening: either it is the mouth of a second pit, such as that by which they let me down, or else it is a natural fissure in the stonery." So I bethought me awhile and nearing the light, found that it came from a breach in the back side of the mountain, which the wild beasts had enlarged by burrowing, that they might enter and devour the dead and freely go to and fro. When I saw this, my spirits revived and hope came back to me and I made sure of life, after having died a death. So I went on, as in a dream, and making shift to scramble through the breach found myself on the slope of a high mountain, overlooking the salt sea and cutting off all access thereto from the island, so that none could come at that part of the beach from the city. [52] I praised my Lord and thanked Him, rejoicing greatly and heartening myself with the prospect of deliverance; then I returned through the crack to the cavern and brought out all the food and water I had saved up and donned some of the dead folk's clothes over my own; after which I gathered together all the collars and necklaces of pearls and jewels and trinkets of gold and silver set with precious stones and other ornaments and valuables I could find upon the corpses; and, making them into bundles with the grave clothes and raiment of the dead, carried them out to the back of the mountain facing the sea-shore, where I established myself, purposing to wait there till it should please Almighty Allah to send me relief by means of some passing ship. I visited the cavern daily and as often as I found folk buried alive there, I killed them all indifferently, men and women, and took their victual and valuables and transported them to my seat on the sea-shore. Thus I abode a long while,—And Shahrazad perceived the dawn of day and ceased saying her permitted say.

When it was the Five Hundred and Fifty-fifth Night,

She said, It hath reached me, O auspicious King, that Sindbad the Seaman continued:—And after carrying all my victuals and valuables from the cavern to the coast I abode a long while by the sea, pondering my case, till one day I caught sight of a ship passing in the midst of the clashing sea, swollen with dashing billows. So I took a piece of a white shroud I had with me and, tying it to a staff, ran along the sea-shore, making signals therewith and calling to the people in the ship, till they espied me and hearing my shouts, sent a boat to fetch me off. When it drew near, the crew called out to me, saying, "Who art thou and how camest thou to be on this mountain, whereon never saw we any in our born days?" I answered, "I am a gentleman [53] and a merchant, who hath been wrecked and saved myself on one of the planks of the ship, with some of my goods; and by the blessing of the Almighty and the decrees of Destiny and my own strength and skill, after much toil and moil I have landed with my gear in this place where I awaited some passing ship to take me off." So they took me in their boat together with the bundles I had made of the jewels and valuables from the cavern, tied up in clothes and shrouds, and rowed back with me to the ship, where the captain said to me, "How camest thou, O man, to yonder place on yonder mountain behind which lieth a great city? All my life I have sailed these seas and passed to and fro hard by these heights; yet never saw I here any living thing save wild beasts and birds." I repeated to him the story I had told the sailors, [54] but acquainted him with nothing of that which had befallen me in the city and the cavern, lest there should be any of the islandry in the ship. Then I took out some of the best pearls I had with me and offered them to the captain, saying, "O my lord, thou hast been the means of saving me off this mountain. I have no ready money; but take this from me in requital of thy kindness and good offices." But he refused to accept it of me, saying, "When we find a shipwrecked man on the sea-shore or on an island, we take him up and give him meat and drink, and if he be naked we clothe him; nor take we aught from him; nay, when we reach a port of safety, we set him ashore with a present of our own money and entreat him kindly and charitably, for the love of Allah the Most High." So I prayed that his life be long in the land and rejoiced in my escape, trusting to be delivered from my stress and to forget my past mishaps; for every time I remembered being let down into the cave with my dead wife I shuddered in horror. Then we pursued our voyage and sailed from island to island and sea to sea, till we arrived at the Island of the Bell, which containeth a city two days' journey in extent, whence after a six days' run we reached the Island Kala, hard by the land of Hind. [55] This place is governed by a potent and puissant King and it produceth excellent camphor and an abundance of the Indian rattan: here also is a lead mine. At last by the decree of Allah, we arrived in safety at Bassorah-town where I tarried a few days, then went on to Baghdad-city, and, finding my quarter, entered my house with lively pleasure. There I foregathered with my family and friends, who rejoiced in my happy return and gave my joy of my safety. I laid up in my storehouses all the goods I had brought with me, and gave alms and largesse to Fakirs and beggars and clothed the widow and the orphan. Then I gave myself up to pleasure and enjoyment, returning to my old merry mode of life. "Such, then, be the most marvellous adventures of my fourth voyage, but to-morrow if you will kindly come to me, I will tell you that which befel me in my fifth voyage, which was yet rarer and more marvellous than those which forewent it. And thou, O my brother Sindbad the Landsman, shalt sup with me as thou art wont." (Saith he who telleth the tale), When Sindbad the Seaman had made an end of his story, he called for supper; so they spread the table and the guests ate the evening meal; after which he gave the Porter an hundred dinars as usual, and he and the rest of the company went their ways, glad at heart and marvelling at the tales they had heard, for that each story was more extraordinary than that which forewent it. The porter Sindbad passed the night in his own house, in all joy and cheer and wonderment; and, as soon as morning came with its sheen and shone, he prayed the dawn-prayer and repaired to the house of Sindbad the Seaman, who welcomed him and bade him sit with him till the rest of the company arrived, when they ate and drank and made merry and the talk went round amongst them. Presently, their host began the narrative of the fifth voyage,—And Shahrazad perceived the dawn of day and ceased to say her permitted say.

When it was the Five Hundred and Fifty-sixth Night,

She said, It hath reached me, O auspicious King, that the host began in these words the narrative of

THE FIFTH VOYAGE OF SINDBAD THE SEAMAN.

Know, O my brothers, that when I had been awhile on shore after my fourth voyage; and when, in my comfort and pleasures and merry-makings and in my rejoicing over my large gains and profits, I had forgotten all I had endured of perils and sufferings, the carnal man was again seized with the longing to travel and to see foreign countries and islands. [56] Accordingly I bought costly merchandise suited to my purpose and, making it up into bales, repaired to Bassorah, where I walked about the river-quay till I found a fine tall ship, newly builded with gear unused and fitted ready for sea. She pleased me; so I bought her and, embarking my goods in her, hired a master and crew, over whom I set certain of my slaves and servants as inspectors. A number of merchants also brought their outfits and paid me freight and passage-money; then, after reciting the Fatihah we set sail over Allah's pool in all joy and cheer, promising ourselves a prosperous voyage and much profit. We sailed from city to city and from island to island and from sea to sea viewing the cities and countries by which we passed, and selling and buying in not a few till one day we came to a great uninhabited island, deserted and desolate, whereon was a white dome of biggest bulk half buried in the sands. The merchants landed to examine this dome, leaving me in the ship; and when they drew near, behold, it was a huge Rukh's egg. They fell a-beating it with stones, knowing not what it was, and presently broke it open, whereupon much water ran out of it and the young Rukh appeared within. So they pulled it forth of the shell and cut its throat and took of it great store of meat. Now I was in the ship and knew not what they did; but presently one of the passengers came up to me and said, "O my lord, come and look at the egg we thought to be a dome." So I looked and seeing the merchants beating it with stones, called out to them, "Stop, stop! do not meddle with that egg, or the bird Rukh will come out and break our ship and destroy us." [57] But they paid no heed to me and gave not over smiting upon the egg, when behold, the day grew dark and dun and the sun was hidden from us, as if some great cloud had passed over the firmament. [58] So we raised our eyes and saw that what we took for a cloud was the Rukh poised between us and the sun, and it was his wings that darkened the day. When he came and saw his egg broken, he cried a loud cry, whereupon his mate came flying up and they both began circling about the ship, crying out at us with voices louder than thunder. I called to the Rais and crew, "Put out to sea and seek safety in flight, before we be all destroyed." So the merchants came on board and we cast off and made haste from the island to gain the open sea. When the Rukhs saw this, they flew off and we crowded all sail on the ship, thinking to get out of their country; but presently the two re-appeared and flew after us and stood over us, each carrying in its claws a huge boulder which it had brought from the mountains. As soon as the he-Rukh came up with us, he let fall upon us the rock he held in his pounces; but the master put about ship, so that the rock missed her by some small matter and plunged into the waves with such violence, that the ship pitched high and then sank into the trough of the sea and the bottom of the ocean appeared to us. Then the she-Rukh let fall her rock, which was bigger than that of her mate, and as Destiny had decreed, it fell on the poop of the ship and crushed it, the rudder flying into twenty pieces; whereupon the vessel foundered and all and everything on board were cast into the main. [59] As for me I struggled for sweet life, till Almighty Allah threw in my way one of the planks of the ship, to which I clung and bestriding it, fell a-paddling with my feet. Now the ship had gone down hard by an island in the midst of the main and the winds and waves bore me on till, by permission of the Most High, they cast me up on the shore of the island, at the last gasp for toil and distress and half dead with hunger and thirst. So I landed more like a corpse than a live man and throwing myself down on the beach, lay there awhile, till I began to revive and recover spirits, when I walked about the island and found it as it were one of the garths and gardens of Paradise. Its trees, in abundance dight, bore ripe-yellow fruit for freight; its streams ran clear and bright; its flowers were fair to scent and to sight and its birds warbled with delight the praises of Him to whom belong permanence and all-might. So I ate my fill of the fruits and slaked my thirst with the water of the streams till I could no more and I returned thanks to the Most High and glorified Him;—And Shahrazad perceived the dawn of day and ceased saying her permitted say.

When it was the Five Hundred and Fifty-seventh Night,

She said, It hath reached me, O auspicious King, that Sindbad the Seaman continued:—So when I escaped drowning and reached the island which afforded me fruit to eat and water to drink, I returned thanks to the Most High and glorified Him; after which I sat till nightfall, hearing no voice and seeing none inhabitant. Then I lay down, well-nigh dead for travail and trouble and terror, and slept without surcease till morning, when I arose and walked about under the trees, till I came to the channel of a draw-well fed by a spring of running water, by which well sat an old man of venerable aspect, girt about with a waist-cloth [60] made of the fibre of palm-fronds. [61] Quoth I to myself, "Haply this Shaykh is one of those who were wrecked in the ship and hath made his way to this island." So I drew near to him and saluted him, and he returned my salam by signs, but spoke not; and I said to him, "O nuncle mine, what causeth thee to sit here?" He shook his head and moaned and signed to me with his hands as who should say, "Take me on thy shoulders and carry me to the other side of the well-channel." And quoth I in my mind, "I will deal kindly with him and do what he desireth; it may be I shall win me a reward in Heaven for he may be a paralytic." So I took him on my back and carrying him to the place whereat he pointed, said to him, "Dismount at thy leisure." But he would not get off my back and wound his legs about my neck. I looked at them and seeing that they were like a buffalo's hide for blackness and roughness, [62] was affrighted and would have cast him off; but he clung to me and gripped my neck with his legs, till I was well-nigh choked, the world grew black in my sight and I fell senseless to the ground like one dead. But he still kept his seat and raising his legs drummed with his heels and beat harder than palm-rods my back and shoulders, till he forced me to rise for excess of pain. Then he signed to me with his hand to carry him hither and thither among the trees which bore the best fruits; and if ever I refused to do his bidding or loitered or took my leisure he beat me with his feet more grievously than if I had been beaten with whips. He ceased not to signal with his hand wherever he was minded to go; so I carried him about the island, like a captive slave, and he bepissed and conskited my shoulders and back, dismounting not night nor day; and whenas he wished to sleep he wound his legs about my neck and leaned back and slept awhile, then arose and beat me; whereupon I sprang up in haste, unable to gainsay him because of the pain he inflicted on me. And indeed I blamed myself and sore repented me of having taken compassion on him and continued in this condition, suffering fatigue not to be described, till I said to myself, "I wrought him a weal and he requited me with my ill; by Allah, never more will I do any man a service so long as I live!" And again and again I besought the Most High that I might die, for stress of weariness and misery; and thus I abode a long while till, one day, I came with him to a place wherein was abundance of gourds, many of them dry. So I took a great dry gourd and, cutting open the head, scooped out the inside and cleaned it; after which I gathered grapes from a vine which grew hard by and squeezed them into the gourd, till it was full of the juice. Then I stopped up the mouth and set it in the sun, where I left it for some days, until it became strong wine; and every day I used to drink of it, to comfort and sustain me under my fatigues with that froward and obstinate fiend; and as often as I drank myself drunk, I forgot my troubles and took new heart. One day he saw me drinking and signed to me with his hand, as who should say, "What is that?" Quoth I, "It is an excellent cordial, which cheereth the heart and reviveth the spirits." Then, being heated with wine, I ran and danced with him among the trees, clapping my hands and singing and making merry; and I staggered under him by design. When he saw this, he signed to me to give him the gourd that he might drink, and I feared him and gave it him. So he took it and, draining it to the dregs, cast it on the ground, whereupon he grew frolicsome and began to clap hands and jig to and fro on my shoulders and he made water upon me so copiously that all my dress was drenched. But presently the fumes of the wine rising to his head, he became helplessly drunk and his side-muscles and limbs relaxed and he swayed to and fro on my back. When I saw that he had lost his senses for drunkenness, I put my hand to his legs and, loosing them from my neck, stooped down well-nigh to the ground and threw him at full length,—And Shahrazad perceived the dawn of day and ceased to say her permitted say.

When it was the Five Hundred and Fifty-eighth Night,

She said, It hath reached me, O auspicious King, that Sindbad the Seaman continued:—So I threw the devil off my shoulders, hardly crediting my deliverance from him and fearing lest he should shake off his drunkenness and do me a mischief. Then I took up a great stone from among the trees and coming up to him smote him therewith on the head with all my might and crushed in his skull as he lay dead drunk. Thereupon his flesh and fat and blood being in a pulp, he died and went to his deserts, The Fire, no mercy of Allah be upon him! I then returned, with a heart at ease, to my former station on the sea-shore and abode in that island many days, eating of its fruits and drinking of its waters and keeping a look-out for passing ships; till one day, as I sat on the beach, recalling all that had befallen me and saying, "I wonder if Allah will save me alive and restore me to my home and family and friends!" behold, a ship was making for the island through the dashing sea and clashing waves. Presently, it cast anchor and the passengers landed; so I made for them, and when they saw me all hastened up to me and gathering round me questioned me of my case and how I came thither. I told them all that had betided me, whereat they marvelled with exceeding marvel and said, "He who rode on thy shoulder is called the 'Shaykh al-Bahr' or Old Man of the Sea, [63] and none ever felt his legs on neck and came off alive but thou; and those who die under him he eateth: so praised be Allah for thy safety!" Then they set somewhat of food before me, whereof I ate my fill, and gave me somewhat of clothes wherewith I clad myself anew and covered my nakedness; after which they took me up into the ship, and we sailed days and nights, till fate brought us to a place called the City of Apes, builded with lofty houses, all of which gave upon the sea and it had a single gate studded and strengthened with iron nails. Now every night, as soon as it is dusk the dwellers in this city use to come forth of the gates and, putting out to sea in boats and ships, pass the night upon the waters in their fear lest the apes should come down on them from the mountains. Hearing this I was sore troubled remembering what I had before suffered from the ape-kind. Presently I landed to solace myself in the city, but meanwhile the ship set sail without me and I repented of having gone ashore, and calling to mind my companions and what had befallen me with the apes, first and after, sat down and fell a-weeping and lamenting. Presently one of the townsfolk accosted me and said to me, "O my lord, meseemeth thou art a stranger to these parts?" "Yes," answered I, "I am indeed a stranger and a poor one, who came hither in a ship which cast anchor here, and I landed to visit the town; but when I would have gone on board again, I found they had sailed without me." Quoth he, "Come and embark with us, for if thou lie the night in the city, the apes will destroy thee." "Hearkening and obedience," replied I, and rising, straightway embarked with him in one of the boats, whereupon they pushed off from shore and anchoring a mile or so from the land, there passed the night. At daybreak, they rowed back to the city and landing, went each about his business. Thus they did every night, for if any tarried in the town by night the apes came down on him and slew him. As soon as it was day, the apes left the place and ate of the fruits of the gardens, then went back to the mountains and slept there till nightfall, when they again came down upon the city. [64] Now this place was in the farthest part of the country of the blacks, and one of the strangest things that befel me during my sojourn in the city was on this wise. One of the company with whom I passed the night in the boat, asked me, "O my lord, thou art apparently a stranger in these parts; hast thou any craft whereat thou canst work?"; and I answered, "By Allah, O my brother, I have no trade nor know I any handicraft, for I was a merchant and a man of money and substance and had a ship of my own, laden with great store of goods and merchandise; but it foundered at sea and all were drowned excepting me who saved myself on a piece of plank which Allah vouchsafed to me of His favour." Upon this he brought me a cotton bag and giving it to me, said, "Take this bag and fill it with pebbles from the beach and go forth with a company of the townsfolk to whom I will give a charge respecting thee. Do as they do and belike thou shalt gain what may further thy return voyage to thy native land." Then he carried me to the beach, where I filled my bag with pebbles large and small, and presently we saw a company of folk issue from the town, each bearing a bag like mine, filled with pebbles. To these he committed me, commending me to their care, and saying, "This man is a stranger, so take him with you and teach him how to gather, that he may get his daily bread, and you will earn your reward and recompense in Heaven." "On our head and eyes be it!" answered they and bidding me welcome, fared on with me till we came to a spacious Wady, full of lofty trees with trunks so smooth that none might climb them. Now sleeping under these trees were many apes, which when they saw us rose and fled from us and swarmed up among the branches; whereupon my companions began to pelt them with what they had in their bags, and the apes fell to plucking of the fruit of the trees and casting them at the folk. I looked at the fruits they cast at us and found them to be Indian [65] or cocoa-nuts; so I chose out a great tree, full of apes, and going up to it, began to pelt them with stones, and they in return pelted me with nuts, which I collected, as did the rest; so that even before I had made an end of my bagful of pebbles, I had gotten great plenty of nuts; and as soon as my companions had in like manner gotten as many nuts as they could carry, we returned to the city, where we arrived at the fag-end of day. Then I went in to the kindly man who had brought me in company with the nut-gatherers and gave him all I had gotten, thanking him for his kindness; but he would not accept them, saying, "Sell them and make profit by the price; and presently he added (giving me the key of a closet in his house) "Store thy nuts in this safe place and go thou forth every morning and gather them as thou hast done to-day, and choose out the worst for sale and supplying thyself; but lay up the rest here, so haply thou mayst collect enough to serve thee for thy return home." "Allah requite thee!" answered I and did as he advised me, going out daily with the cocoa-nut gatherers, who commended me to one another and showed me the best-stocked trees. [66] Thus did I for some time, till I had laid up great store of excellent nuts, besides a large sum of money, the price of those I had sold. I became thus at my ease and bought all I saw and had a mind to, and passed my time pleasantly greatly enjoying my stay in the city, till, as I stood on the beach, one day, a great ship steering through the heart of the sea presently cast anchor by the shore and landed a company of merchants, who proceeded to sell and buy and barter their goods for cocoa-nuts and other commodities. Then I went to my friend and told him of the coming of the ship and how I had a mind to return to my own country; and he said, "'Tis for thee to decide." So I thanked him for his bounties and took leave of him; then, going to the captain of the ship, I agreed with him for my passage and embarked my cocoa-nuts and what else I possessed. We weighed anchor,—And Shahrazad perceived the dawn of day and ceased saying her permitted say.

When it was the Five Hundred and Fifty-ninth Night,

She said, It hath reached me, O auspicious King, that Sindbad the Seaman continued:—So I left the City of the Apes and embarked my cocoa-nuts and what else I possessed. We weighed anchor the same day and sailed from island to island and sea to sea; and whenever we stopped, I sold and traded with my cocoa-nuts, and the Lord requited me more than I erst had and lost. Amongst other places, we came to an island abounding in cloves [67] and cinnamon and pepper; and the country people told me that by the side of each pepper-bunch groweth a great leaf which shadeth it from the sun and casteth the water off it in the wet season; but, when the rain ceaseth the leaf turneth over and droopeth down by the side of the bunch. [68] Here I took in great store of pepper and cloves and cinnamon, in exchange for cocoa-nuts, and we passed thence to the Island of Al-Usirat, [69] whence cometh the Comorin aloes-wood and thence to another island, five days' journey in length, where grows the Chinese lign-aloes, which is better than the Comorin; but the people of this island [70] are fouler of condition and religion than those of the other, for that they love fornication and wine-bibbing, and know not prayer nor call to prayer. Thence we came to the pearl-fisheries, and I gave the divers some of my cocoa-nuts and said to them, "Dive for my luck and lot!" They did so and brought up from the deep bight [71] great store of large and priceless pearls; and they said to me, "By Allah, O my master, thy luck is a lucky!" Then we sailed on, with the blessing of Allah (whose name be exalted!); and ceased not sailing till we arrived safely at Bassorah. There I abode a little and then went on to Baghdad, where I entered my quarter and found my house and foregathered with my family and saluted my friends who gave me joy of my safe return, and I laid up all my goods and valuables in my storehouses. Then I distributed alms and largesse and clothed the widow and the orphan and made presents to my relations and comrades; for the Lord had requited me fourfold that I had lost. After which I returned to my old merry way of life and forgot all I had suffered in the great profit and gain I had made. "Such, then, is the history of my fifth voyage and its wonderments, and now to supper; and to-morrow, come again and I will tell you what befel me in my sixth voyage; for it was still more wonderful than this." (Saith he who telleth the tale), Then he called for food; and the servants spread the table, and when they had eaten the evening-meal, he bade give Sindbad the porter an hundred golden dinars and the Landsman returned home and lay him down to sleep, much marvelling at all he had heard. Next morning, as soon as it was light, he prayed the dawn-prayer; and, after blessing Mohammed the Cream of all creatures, betook himself to the house of Sindbad the Seaman and wished him a good day. The merchant bade him sit and talked with him, till the rest of the company arrived. Then the servants spread the table and when they had well eaten and drunken and were mirthful and merry, Sindbad the Seaman began in these words the narrative of

THE SIXTH VOYAGE OF SINDBAD THE SEAMAN.

Know, O my brothers and friends and companions all, that I abode some time, after my return from my fifth voyage, in great solace and satisfaction and mirth and merriment, joyance and enjoyment; and I forgot what I had suffered, seeing the great gain and profit I had made till, one day, as I sat making merry and enjoying myself with my friends, there came in to me a company of merchants whose case told tales of travel, and talked with me of voyage and adventure and greatness of pelf and lucre. Hereupon I remembered the days of my return from abroad, and my joy at once more seeing my native land and foregathering with my family and friends; and my soul yearned for travel and traffic. So compelled by Fate and Fortune I resolved to undertake another voyage; and, buying me fine and costly merchandise meet for foreign trade, made it up into bales, with which I journeyed from Baghdad to Bassorah. Here I found a great ship ready for sea and full of merchants and notables, who had with them goods of price; so I embarked my bales therein. And we left Bassorah in safety and good spirits under the safeguard of the King, the Preserver.—And Shahrazad perceived the dawn of day and ceased to say her permitted say.

When it was the Five Hundred and Sixtieth Night,

She said, It hath reached me, O auspicious King, that Sindbad the Seaman continued:—And after embarking my bales and leaving Bassorah in safety and good spirits, we continued our voyage from place to place and from city to city, buying and selling and profiting and diverting ourselves with the sight of countries where strange folk dwell. And Fortune and the voyage smiled upon us, till one day, as we went along, behold, the captain suddenly cried with a great cry and cast his turband on the deck. Then he buffeted his face like a woman and plucked out his beard and fell down in the waist of the ship will nigh fainting for stress of grief and rage, and crying, "Oh and alas for the ruin of my house and the orphanship of my poor children!" So all the merchant and sailors came round about him and asked him, "O master, what is the matter?"; for the light had become night before their sight. And he answered, saying, "Know, O folk, that we have wandered from our course and left the sea whose ways we wot, and come into a sea whose ways I know not; and unless Allah vouchsafe us a means of escape, we are all dead men; wherefore pray ye to the Most High, that He deliver us from this strait. Haply amongst you is one righteous whose prayers the Lord will accept." Then he arose and clomb the mast to see an there were any escape from that strait; and he would have loosed the sails; but the wind redoubled upon the ship and whirled her round thrice and drave her backwards; whereupon her rudder brake and she fell off towards a high mountain. With this the captain came down from the mast, saying, "There is no Majesty and there is no Might save in Allah, the Glorious, the Great; nor can man prevent that which is fore-ordained of fate! By Allah, we are fallen on a place of sure destruction, and there is no way of escape for us, nor can any of us be saved!" Then we all fell a-weeping over ourselves and bidding one another farewell for that our days were come to an end, and we had lost all hopes of life. Presently the ship struck the mountain and broke up, and all and everything on board of her were plunged into the sea. Some of the merchants were drowned and others made shift to reach the shore and save themselves upon the mountain; I amongst the number, and when we got ashore, we found a great island, or rather peninsula [72] whose base was strewn with wreckage of crafts and goods and gear cast up by the sea from broken ships whose passengers had been drowned; and the quantity confounded compt and calculation. So I climbed the cliffs into the inward of the isle and walked on inland, till I came to a stream of sweet water, that welled up at the nearest foot of the mountains and disappeared in the earth under the range of hills on the opposite side. But all the other passengers went over the mountains to the inner tracts; and, dispersing hither and thither, were confounded at what they saw and became like madmen at the sight of the wealth and treasures wherewith the shores were strewn. As for me I looked into the bed of the stream aforesaid and saw therein great plenty of rubies, and great royal pearls [73] and all kinds of jewels and precious stones which were as gravel in the bed of the rivulets that ran through the fields, and the sands sparkled and glittered with gems and precious ores. Moreover we found in the island abundance of the finest lign-aloes, both Chinese and Comorin; and there also is a spring of crude ambergris [74] which floweth like wax or gum over the stream-banks, for the great heat of the sun, and runneth down to the sea-shore, where the monsters of the deep come up and swallowing it, return into the sea.

But it burneth in their bellies; so they cast it up again and it congealeth on the surface of the water, whereby its color and quantities are changed; and at last, the waves cast it ashore, and the travellers and merchants who know it, collect it and sell it. But as to the raw ambergris which is not swallowed, it floweth over the channel and congealeth on the banks and when the sun shineth on it, it melteth and scenteth the whole valley with a musk-like fragrance: then, when the sun ceaseth from it, it congealeth again. But none can get to this place where is the crude ambergris, because of the mountains which enclose the island on all sides and which foot of man cannot ascend. [75] We continued thus to explore the island, marvelling at the wonderful works of Allah and the riches we found there, but sore troubled for our own case, and dismayed at our prospects. Now we had picked up on the beach some small matter of victual from the wreck and husbanded it carefully, eating but once every day or two, in our fear lest it should fail us and we die miserably of famine or affright. Moreover, we were weak for colic brought on by sea-sickness and low diet, and my companions deceased, one after other, till there was but a small company of us left. Each that died we washed and shrouded in some of the clothes and linen cast ashore by the tides; and after a little, the rest of my fellows perished, one by one, till I had buried the last of the party and abode alone on the island, with but a little provision left, I who was wont to have so much. And I wept over myself, saying, "Would Heaven I had died before my companions and they had washed and buried me! It had been better than I should perish and none wash me and shroud me and bury me. But there is Majesty and there is no Might save in Allah, the Glorious, the Great!"—And Shahrazad perceived the dawn of day and ceased saying her permitted say.

When it was the Five Hundred and Sixty-first Night,

She said, It hath reached me, O auspicious King, that Sindbad the Seaman continued in these words:—Now after I had buried the last of my party and abode alone on the island, I arose and dug me a deep grave on the sea-shore, saying to myself, "Whenas I grow weak and know that death cometh to me, I will cast myself into the grave and die there, so the wind may drift the sand over me and cover me and I be buried therein." [76] Then I fell to reproaching myself for my little wit in leaving my native land and betaking me again to travel, after all I had suffered during my first five voyages, and when I had not made a single one without suffering more horrible perils and more terrible hardships than in its forerunner and having no hope of escape from my present stress; and I repented me of my folly and bemoaned myself, especially as I had no need of money, seeing that I had enough and more than enough and could not spend what I had, no, nor a half of it in all my life. However, after a while Allah sent me a thought and I said to myself, "By God, needs must this stream have an end as well as a beginning; ergo an issue somewhere, and belike its course may lead to some inhabited place; so my best plan is to make me a little boat [77] big enough to sit in, and carry it and launching it on the river, embark therein and drop down the stream. If I escape, I escape, by God's leave; and if I perish, better die in the river than here." Then, sighing for myself, I set to work collecting a number of pieces of Chinese and Comorin aloes-wood and I bound them together with ropes from the wreckage; then I chose out from the broken-up ships straight planks of even size and fixed them firmly upon the aloes-wood, making me a boat-raft a little narrower than the channel of the stream; and I tied it tightly and firmly as though it were nailed. Then I loaded it with the goods, precious ores and jewels: and the union pearls which were like gravel and the best of the ambergris crude and pure, together with what I had collected on the island and what was left me of victual and wild herbs. Lastly I lashed a piece of wood on either side, to serve me as oars; and launched it, and embarking, did according to the saying of the poet,

> "Fly, fly with life whenas evils threat;
> Leave the house to tell of its builder's fate!
> Land after land shalt thou seek and find
> But no other life on thy wish shall wait:
> Fret not thy soul in thy thoughts o' night;
> All woes shall end or sooner or late.
> Whoso is born in one land to die,
> There and only there shall gang his gait:
> Nor trust great things to another wight,
> Soul hath only soul for confederate." [78]

My boat-raft drifted with the stream, I pondering the issue of my affair; and the drifting ceased not till I came to the place where it disappeared beneath the mountain. I rowed my conveyance into the place which was intensely dark; and the current carried the raft with it down the underground channel. [79] The thin stream bore me on through a narrow tunnel where the raft touched either side and my head rubbed against the roof, return therefrom being impossible. Then I blamed myself for having thus risked my life, and said, "If this passage grow any straiter, the raft will hardly pass, and I cannot turn back; so I shall inevitably perish miserably in this place." And I threw myself down upon my face on the raft, by reason of the narrowness of the channel, whilst the stream ceased not to carry me along, knowing not night from day, for the excess of the gloom which encompassed me about and my terror and concern for myself lest I should perish. And in such condition my course continued down the channel which now grew wide and then straiter till, sore aweary by reason of the darkness which could be felt, I fell asleep, as I lay prone on the raft, and I slept knowing not an the time were long or short. When I awoke at last, I found myself in the light of Heaven and opening my eyes I saw myself in a broad stream and the raft moored to an island in the midst of a number of Indians and Abyssinians. As soon as these blackamoors [80] saw that I was awake, they came up to me and bespoke me in their speech; but I understood not what they said and thought that this was a dream and a vision which had betided me for stress of concern and chagrin. But I was delighted at my escape from the river. When they saw I understood them not and made them no answer, one of them came forward and said to me in Arabic, "Peace be with thee, O my brother! Who art thou and whence faredst thou thither? How camest thou into this river and what manner of land lies behind yonder mountains, for never knew we any one make his way thence to us?" Quoth I, "And upon thee be peace and the ruth of Allah and his blessing! Who are ye and what country is this?" "O my brother," answered he, "we are husbandmen and tillers of the soil, who came out to water our fields and plantations; and, finding thee asleep on this raft, laid hold of it and made it fast by us, against thou shouldst awake at thy leisure. So tell us how thou camest hither?" I answered, "For Allah's sake, O my lord, ere I speak give me somewhat to eat, for I am starving, and after ask me what thou wilt." So he hastened to fetch me food and I ate my fill, till I was refreshed and my fear was calmed by a good belly-full and my life returned to me. Then I rendered thanks to the Most High for mercies great and small, glad to be out of the river and rejoicing to be amongst them, and I told them all my adventures from first to last, especially my troubles in the narrow channel.—And Shahrazad perceived the dawn of day and ceased to say her permitted say.

When it was the Five Hundred and Sixty-second Night,

She said, It hath reached me, O auspicious King, that Sindbad the Seaman continued:—When I landed and found myself amongst the Indians and Abyssinians and had taken some rest, they consulted among themselves and said to one another, "There is no help for it but we carry him with us and present him to our King, that he may acquaint him with his adventures." So they took me, together with the raft-boat and its lading of monies and merchandise; jewels, minerals and golden gear, and brought me to their King, who was King of Sarandib, [81] telling him what had happened; whereupon he saluted me and bade me welcome. Then he questioned me of my condition and adventures through the man who had spoken Arabic and I repeated to him my story from beginning to end, whereat he marvelled exceedingly and gave me joy of my deliverance; after which I arose and fetched from the raft great store of precious ores and jewels and ambergris and lign-aloes and presented them to the King, who accepted them and entreated me with the utmost honour, appointing me a lodging in his own palace. So I consorted with the chief of the islanders, and they paid me the utmost respect. And I quitted not the royal palace. Now the Island Sarandib lieth under the equinoctial line, its night and day both numbering twelve house. It measureth eighty leagues long by a breadth of thirty and its width is bounded by a lofty mountain [82] and a deep valley, The mountain is conspicuous from a distance of three days and it containeth many kinds of rubies and other minerals, and spice-trees of all sorts. The surface is covered with emery wherewith gems are cut and fashioned; diamonds are in its rivers and pearls are in its valleys. I ascended that mountain and solaced myself with a view of its marvels which are indescribable and afterwards I returned to the King. [83] Thereupon, all the travellers and merchants who came to the place questioned me of the affairs of my native land and of the Caliph Harun al-Rashid and his rule and I told them of him and of that wherefor he was renowned, and they praised him because of this; whilst I in turn questioned them of the manners and customs of their own countries and got the knowledge I desired. One day, the King himself asked me of the fashions and form of government of my country, and I acquainted him with the circumstance of the Caliph's sway in the city of Baghdad and the justice of his rule. The King marvelled at my account of his appointments and said, "By Allah, the Caliph's ordinances are indeed wise and his fashions of praiseworthy guise and thou hast made me love him by what thou tellest me; wherefore I have a mind to make him a present and send it by thee." Quoth I, "Hearkening and obedience, O my lord; I will bear thy gift to him and inform him that thou art his sincere lover and true friend." Then I abode with the King in great honour and regard and consideration for a long while till, one day, as I sat in his palace, I heard news of a company of merchants, that were fitting out a ship for Bassorah, and said to myself,

"I cannot do better than voyage with these men." So I rose without stay or delay and kissed the King's hand and acquainted him with my longing to set out with the merchants, for that I pined after my people and mine own land. Quoth he, "Thou art thine own master; yet, if it be thy will to abide with us, on our head and eyes be it, for thou gladdenest us with thy company." "By Allah, O my lord," answered I, "thou hast indeed overwhelmed me with thy favours and well-doings; but I weary for a sight of my friends and family and native country." When he heard this, he summoned the merchants in question and commended me to their care, paying my freight and passage-money. Then he bestowed on me great riches from his treasuries and charged me with a magnificent present for the Caliph Harun al-Rashid. Moreover he gave me a sealed letter, saying, "Carry this with thine own hand to the Commander of the Faithful and give him many salutations from us!" "Hearing and obedience," I replied. The missive was written on the skin of the Kháwi [84] (which is finer than lamb-parchment and of yellow colour), with ink of ultramarine and the contents were as follows. "Peace be with thee from the King of Al-Hind, before whom are a thousand elephants and upon whose palace-crenelles are a thousand jewels. But after (laud to the Lord and praises to His Prophet!): we send thee a trifling gift which be thou pleased to accept. Thou art to us a brother and a sincere friend; and great is the love we bear for thee in heart; favour us therefore with a reply. The gift besitteth not thy dignity: but we beg of thee, O our brother, graciously to accept it and peace be with thee." And the present was a cup of ruby a span high [85] the inside of which was adorned with precious pearls; and a bed covered with the skin of the serpent which swalloweth the elephant, which skin hath spots each like a dinar and whoso sitteth upon it never sickeneth; [86] and an hundred thousand miskals of Indian lign-aloes and a slave-girl like a shining moon. Then I took leave of him and of all my intimates and acquaintances in the island and embarked with the merchants aforesaid. We sailed with a fair wind, committing ourselves to the care of Allah (be He extolled and exalted!) and by His permission arrived at Bassorah, where I passed a few days and nights equipping myself and packing up my bales. Then I went on to Baghdad-city, the House of Peace, where I sought an audience of the Caliph and laid the King's presents before him. He asked me whence they came and I said to him, "By Allah, O Commander of the Faithful, I know not the name of the city nor the way thither!" He then asked me, "O Sindbad, is this true which the King writeth?"; and I answered, after kissing the ground, "O my lord, I saw in his kingdom much more than he hath written in his letter. For state processions a throne is set for him upon a huge elephant, eleven cubits high: and upon this he sitteth having his great lords and officers and guests standing in two ranks, on his right hand and on his left. At his head is a man hending in hand a golden javelin and behind him another with a great mace of gold whose head is an emerald [87] a span long and as thick as a man's thumb. And when he mounteth horse there mount with him a thousand horsemen clad in gold brocade and silk; and as the King proceedeth a man precedeth him, crying, 'This is the King of great dignity, of high authority!' And he continueth to repeat his praises in words I remember not, saying at the end of his panegyric, 'This is the King owning the crown whose like nor Solomon nor the Mihraj [88] ever possessed.' Then he is silent and one behind him proclaimeth, saying, 'He will die! Again I say he will die!;' and the other addeth, 'Extolled be the perfection of the Living who dieth not!' [89] Moreover by reason of his justice and ordinance and intelligence, there is no Kazi in his city, and all his lieges distinguish between Truth and Falsehood." Quoth the Caliph, "How great is this King! His letter hath shown me this; and as for the mightiness of his dominion thou hast told us what thou hast eye-witnessed. By Allah, he hath been endowed with wisdom as with wide rule." Then I related to the Commander of the Faithful all that had befallen me in my last voyage; at which he wondered exceedingly and bade his historians record my story and store it up in his treasuries, for the edification of all who might see it. Then he conferred on me exceeding great favours, and I repaired to my quarter and entered my home, where I warehoused all my goods and possessions. Presently, my friends came to me and I distributed presents among my family and gave alms and largesse; after which I yielded myself to joyance and enjoyment, mirth and merry-making, and forgot all that I had suffered. "Such, then, O my brothers, is the history of what befel me in my sixth voyage, and to-morrow, Inshallah! I will tell you the story of my seventh and last voyage, which is still more wondrous and marvellous than that of the first six." (Saith he who telleth the tale), Then he bade lay the table, and the company supped with him; after which he gave the Porter an hundred dinars, as of wont, and they all went their ways, marvelling beyond measure at that which they had heard.—And Shahrazad perceived the dawn of day and ceased saying her permitted say.

When it was the Five Hundred and Sixty-third Night,

She said, It hath reached me, O auspicious King, that when Sindbad the Seaman had related the history of what befel him in his sixth voyage, and all the company had dispersed, Sindbad the Landsman went home and slept as of wont. Next day he rose and prayed the dawn-prayer and repaired to his namesake's house where, after the company was all assembled, the host began to relate

THE SEVENTH VOYAGE OF SINDBAD THE SEAMAN.

Know, O company, that after my return from my sixth voyage, which brought me abundant profit, I resumed my former life in all possible joyance and enjoyment and mirth and making merry day and night; and I tarried some time in this solace and satisfaction till my soul began once more to long to sail the seas and see foreign countries and company with merchants and hear new things. So having made up my mind, I packed up in bales a quantity of precious stuffs suited for sea-trade and repaired with them from Baghdad-city to Bassorah-town, where I found a ship ready for sea, and in her a company of considerable merchants. I shipped with them and becoming friends, we set forth on our venture, in health and safety; and sailed with a fair wind, till we came to a city called Madínat-al-Sín; but after we had left it, as we fared on in all cheer and confidence, devising of traffic and travel, behold, there sprang up a violent head-wind and a tempest of rain fell on us and drenched us and our goods. So we covered the bales with our cloaks and garments and drugget and canvas, lest they be spoiled by the rain, and betook ourselves to prayer and supplication to Almighty Allah and humbled ourselves before Him for deliverance from the peril that was upon us. But the captain arose and tightening his girdle tucked up his skirts and, after taking refuge with Allah from Satan the Stoned, clomb to the mast-head, whence he looked out right and left and gazing at the passengers and crew fell to buffeting his face and plucking out his beard. So we cried to him, "O Rais, what is the matter?"; and he replied saying, "Seek ye deliverance of the Most High from the strait into which we have fallen and bemoan yourselves and take leave of one another; for know that the wind hath gotten the mastery of us and hath driven us into the uttermost of the seas of the world." Then he came down from the mast-head and opening his sea-chest, pulled out a bag of blue cotton, from which he took a powder like ashes. This he set in a saucer wetted with a little water and, after waiting a short time, smelt and tasted it; and then he took out of the chest a booklet, wherein he read awhile and said weeping, "Know, O ye passengers, that in this book is a marvellous matter, denoting that whoso cometh hither shall surely die, without hope of escape; for that this ocean is called the Sea of the Clime of the King, wherein is the sepulchre of our lord Solomon, son of David (on both be peace!) and therein are serpents of vast bulk and fearsome aspect: and what ship soever cometh to these climes there riseth to her a great fish [90] out of the sea and swalloweth her up with all and everything on board her." Hearing these words from the captain great was our wonder, but hardly had he made an end of speaking, when the ship was lifted out of the water and let fall again and we applied to praying the death-prayer [91] and committing our souls to Allah. Presently we heard a terrible great cry like the loud-pealing thunder, whereat we were terror-struck and became as dead men, giving ourselves up for lost. Then behold, there came up to us a huge fish, as big as a tall mountain, at whose sight we became wild for affright and, weeping sore, made ready for death, marvelling at its vast size and gruesome semblance; when lo! a second fish made its appearance than which we had seen naught more monstrous. So we bemoaned ourselves of our lives and farewelled one another; but suddenly up came a third fish bigger than the two first; whereupon we lost the power of thought and reason and were stupefied for the excess of our fear and horror. Then the three fish began circling round about the ship and the third and biggest opened his mouth to swallow it, and we looked into its mouth and behold, it was wider than the gate of a city and its throat was like a long valley. So we besought the Almighty and called for succour upon His Apostle (on whom be blessing and peace!), when suddenly a violent squall of wind arose and smote the ship, which rose out of the water and settled upon a great reef, the haunt of sea-monsters, where it broke up and fell asunder into planks and all and everything on board were plunged into the sea. As for me, I tore off all my clothes but my gown and swam a little way, till I happened upon one of the ship's planks whereto I clung and bestrode it like a horse, whilst the winds and the waters sported with me and the waves carried me up and cast me down; and I was in most piteous plight for fear and distress and hunger and thirst. Then I reproached myself for what I had done and my soul was weary after a life of ease and comfort; and I said to myself, "O Sindbad, O Seaman, thou repentest not and yet thou art ever suffering hardships and travails; yet wilt thou not renounce sea-travel; or, an thou say, 'I renounce,' thou liest in thy renouncement. Endure then with patience that which thou sufferest, for verily thou deservest all that betideth thee!"—And

Shahrazad perceived the dawn of day and ceased to say her permitted say.

When it was the Five Hundred and Sixty-fourth Night,

She said, It hath reached me, O auspicious King, that Sindbad the Seaman continued:—But when I had bestridden the plank, quoth I to myself, "Thou deservest all that betideth thee. All this is decreed to me of Allah (whose name be exalted!), to turn me from my greed of gain, whence ariseth all that I endure, for I have wealth galore." Then I returned to my senses and said, "In very sooth, this time I repent to the Most High, with a sincere repentance, of my lust for gain and venture; and never will I again name travel with tongue nor in thought." And I ceased not to humble myself before Almighty Allah and weep and bewail myself, recalling my former estate of solace and satisfaction and mirth and merriment and joyance; and thus I abode two days, at the end of which time I came to a great island abounding in trees and streams. There I landed and ate of the fruits of the island and drank of its waters, till I was refreshed and my life returned to me and my strength and spirits were restored and I recited,

"Oft when thy case shows knotty and tangled skein,
Fate downs from Heaven and straightens every ply:
In patience keep thy soul till clear thy lot
For He who ties the knot can eke untie."

Then I walked about, till I found on the further side, a great river of sweet water, running with a strong current; whereupon I called to mind the boat-raft I had made aforetime and said to myself, "Needs must I make another; haply I may free me from this strait. If I escape, I have my desire and I vow to Allah Almighty to foreswear travel; and if I perish I shall be at peace and shall rest from toil and moil." So I rose up and gathered together great store of pieces of wood from the trees (which were all of the finest sanders-wood, whose like is not albe I knew it not), and made shift to twist creepers and tree-twigs into a kind of rope, with which I bound the billets together and so contrived a raft. Then saying, "An I be saved, 'tis of God's grace," I embarked thereon and committed myself to the current, and it bore me on for the first day and the second and the third after leaving the island; whilst I lay in the raft, eating not and drinking, when I was athirst, of the water of the river, till I was weak and giddy as a chicken, for stress of fatigue and famine and fear. At the end of this time I came to a high mountain, whereunder ran the river; which when I saw, I feared for my life by reason of the straitness I had suffered in my former journey, and I would fain have stayed the raft and landed on the mountain-side; but the current overpowered me and drew it into the subterranean passage like an archway; whereupon I gave myself up for lost and said, "There is no Majesty and there is no Might save in Allah, the Glorious, the Great!" However, after a little, the raft glided into open air and I saw before me a wide valley, whereinto the river fell with a noise like the rolling of thunder and a swiftness as the rushing of the wind. I held on to the raft, for fear of falling off it, whilst the waves tossed me right and left; and the craft continued to descend with the current nor could I avail to stop it nor turn it shorewards, till it stopped with me at a great and goodly city, grandly edified and containing much people. And when the townsfolk saw me on the raft, dropping down with the current, they threw me out ropes which I had not strength enough to hold; then they tossed a net over the craft and drew it ashore with me, whereupon I fell to the ground amidst them, as I were a dead man, for stress of fear and hunger and lack of sleep. After awhile, there came up to me out of the crowd an old man of reverend aspect, well stricken in years, who welcomed me and threw over me abundance of handsome clothes, wherewith I covered my nakedness. Then he carried me to the Hammam-bath and brought me cordial sherbets and delicious perfumes; moreover, when I came out, he bore me to his house, where his people made much of me and, seating me in a pleasant place, set rich food before me, whereof I ate my fill and returned thanks to God the Most High for my deliverance. Thereupon his pages fetched me hot water, and I washed my hands, and his handmaids brought me silken napkins, with which I dried them and wiped my mouth. Also the Shaykh set apart for me an apartment in a part of his house and charged his pages and slave-girls to wait upon me and do my will and supply my wants. They were assiduous in my service, and I abode with him in the guest-chamber three days, taking my ease of good eating and good drinking and good scents till life returned to me and my terrors subsided and my heart was calmed and my mind was eased. On the fourth day the Shaykh, my host, came in to me and said, "Thou cheerest us with thy company, O my son, and praised be Allah for thy safety! Say: wilt thou now come down with me to the beach and the bazar and sell thy goods and take their price? Belike thou mayst buy thee wherewithal to traffic. I have ordered my servants to remove thy stock-in-trade from the sea and they have piled it on the shore." I was silent awhile and said to myself, "What mean these words and what goods have I?" Then said he, "O my son, be not troubled nor careful, but come with me to the market and if any offer for thy goods what price contenteth thee, take it; but, an thou be not satisfied, I will lay them up for thee in my warehouse, against a fitting occasion for sale." So I bethought me of my case and said to myself, "Do his bidding and see what are these goods!"; and I said to him, "O my nuncle the Shaykh, I hear and I obey; I may not gainsay thee in aught for Allah's blessing is on all thou dost." Accordingly he guided me to the market-street, where I found that he had taken in pieces the raft which carried me and which was of sandal-wood and I heard the broker calling it for sale.—And Shahrazad perceived the dawn of day and ceased saying her permitted say.

When it was the Five Hundred and Sixty-fifth Night,

She said, It hath reached me, O auspicious King, that Sindbad the Seaman thus resumed his tale:—I found that the Shaykh had taken to pieces my raft which lay on the beach and the broker was crying the sandal-wood for sale. Then the merchants came and opened the gate of bidding for the wood and bid against one another till its price reached a thousand dinars, when they left bidding and my host said to me, "Hear, O my son, this is the current price of thy goods in hard times like these: wilt thou sell them for this or shall I lay them up for thee in my storehouses, till such time as prices rise?" "O my lord," answered I, "the business is in thy hands: do as thou wilt." Then asked he, "Wilt thou sell the wood to me, O my son, for an hundred gold pieces over and above what the merchants have bidden for it?" and I answered, "Yes, I have sold it to thee for monies received." [92] So, he bade his servants transport the wood to his storehouses and, carrying me back to his house, seated me and counted out to me the purchase money; after which he laid it in bags and setting them in a privy place, locked them up with an iron padlock and gave me its key. Some days after this, the Shaykh said to me, "O my son, I have somewhat to propose to thee, wherein I trust thou wilt do my bidding." Quoth I, "What is it?" Quoth he, "I am a very old man and have no son; but I have a daughter who is young in years and fair of favour and endowed with abounding wealth and beauty. Now I have a mind to marry her to thee, that thou mayst abide with her in this our country, and I will make thee master of all I have in hand for I am an old man and thou shalt stand in my stead." I was silent for shame and made him no answer, whereupon he continued, "Do my desire in this, O my son, for I wish but thy weal; and if thou wilt but do as I say, thou shalt have her at once and be as my son; and all that is under my hand or that cometh to me shall be thine. If thou have a mind to traffic and travel to thy native land, none shall hinder thee, and thy property will be at thy sole disposal; so do as thou wilt." "By Allah, O my uncle," replied I, "thou art become to me even as my father, and I am a stranger and have undergone many hardships: while for stress of that which I have suffered naught of judgment or knowledge is left to me. It is for thee, therefore, to decide what I shall do." Hereupon he sent his servants for the Kazi and the witnesses and married me to his daughter making us for a noble marriage-feast [93] and high festival. When I went in to her, I found her perfect in beauty and loveliness and symmetry and grace, clad in rich raiment and covered with a profusion of ornaments and necklaces and other trinkets of gold and silver and precious stones, worth a mint of money, a price none could pay. She pleased me and we loved each other; and I abode with her in solace and delight of life, till her father was taken to the mercy of Allah Almighty. So we shrouded him and buried him, and I laid hands on the whole of his property and all his servants and slaves became mine. Moreover, the merchants installed me in his office, for he was their Shaykh and their Chief; and none of them purchased aught but with his knowledge and by his leave. And now his rank passed on to me. When I became acquainted with the townsfolk, I found that at the beginning of each month they were transformed, in that their faces changed and they became like birds and they put forth wings wherewith they flew unto the upper regions of the firmament and none remained in the city save the women and children; and I said in my mind, "When the first of the month cometh, I will ask one of them to carry me with them, whither they go." So when the time came and their complexion changed and their forms altered, I went in to one of the townsfolk and said to him, "Allah upon thee! carry me with thee, that I might divert myself with the rest and return with you." "This may not be," answered he; but I ceased not to solicit him and I importuned him till he consented. Then I went out in his company, without telling any of my family [94] or servants or friends, and he took me on his back and flew up with me so high in air, that I heard the angels glorifying God in the heavenly dome, whereat I wondered and exclaimed, "Praised be Allah! Extolled be the perfection of Allah!" Hardly had I made an end of pronouncing the Tasbih—praised be Allah!—when there came out a fire from heaven and all but consumed the company; whereupon they fled from it and descended with curses upon me and, casting me down on a high mountain, went away, exceeding wroth with me, and left me there alone. As I found myself in this plight, I repented of what I had done and reproached myself for having undertaken that for which I was unable, saying, "There is no

Majesty and there is no Might, save in Allah, the Glorious, the Great! No sooner am I delivered from one affliction than I fall into a worse." And I continued in this case knowing not whither I should go, when lo! there came up two young men, as they were moons, each using as a staff a rod of red gold. So I approached them and saluted them; and when they returned my salam, I said to them, "Allah upon you twain; who are ye and what are ye?" Quoth they, "We are of the servants of the Most High Allah, abiding in this mountain;" and, giving me a rod of red gold they had with them, went their ways and left me. I walked on along the mountain-ridge staying my steps with the staff and pondering the case of the two youths, when behold, a serpent came forth from under the mountain, with a man in her [95] jaws, whom she had swallowed even to below his navel, and he was crying out and saying, "Whoso delivereth me, Allah will deliver him from all adversity!" So I went up to the serpent and smote her on the head with the golden staff, whereupon she cast the man forth of her mouth.—And Shahrazad perceived the dawn of day and ceased to say her permitted say.

When it was the Five Hundred and Sixty-sixth Night,

She said, It hath reached me, O auspicious King, that Sindbad the Seaman thus continued:—When I smote the serpent on the head with my golden staff she cast the man forth of her mouth. Then I smote her a second time, and she turned and fled; whereupon he came up to me and said, "Since my deliverance from yonder serpent hath been at thy hands I will never leave thee, and thou shalt be my comrade on this mountain." "And welcome," answered I; so we fared on along the mountain, till we fell in with a company of folk, and I looked and saw amongst them the very man who had carried me and cast me down there. I went up to him and spake him fair, excusing myself to him and saying, "O my comrade, it is not thus that friend should deal with friend." Quoth he, "It was thou who well-nigh destroyed us by thy Tasbih and thy glorifying God on my back." Quoth I, "Pardon me, for I had no knowledge of this matter; but, if thou wilt take me with thee, I swear not to say a word." So he relented and consented to carry me with him, but he made an express condition that, so long as I abode on his back, I should abstain from pronouncing the Tasbih or otherwise glorifying God. Then I gave the wand of gold to him whom I had delivered from the serpent and bade him farewell, and my friend took me on his back and flew with me as before, till he brought me to the city and set me down in my own house. My wife came to meet me and saluting me gave me joy of my safety and then said, "Beware of going forth hereafter with yonder folk, neither consort with them, for they are brethren of the devils, and know not how to mention the name of Allah Almighty; neither worship they Him." "And how did thy father with them?" asked I; and she answered, "My father was not of them, neither did he as they; and as now he is dead methinks thou hadst better sell all we have and with the price buy merchandise and journey to thine own country and people, and I with thee; for I care not to tarry in this city, my father and my mother being dead." So I sold all the Shaykh's property piecemeal, and looked for one who should be journeying thence to Bassorah that I might join myself to him. And while thus doing I heard of a company of townsfolk who had a mind to make the voyage, but could not find them a ship; so they bought wood and built them a great ship wherein I took passage with them, and paid them all the hire. Then we embarked, I and my wife, with all our moveables, leaving our houses and domains and so forth, and set sail, and ceased not sailing from island to island and from sea to sea, with a fair wind and a favouring, till we arrived at Bassorah safe and sound. I made no stay there, but freighted another vessel and, transferring my goods to her, set out forthright for Baghdad-city, where I arrived in safety, and entering my quarter and repairing to my house, foregathered with my family and friends and familiars who laid up my goods in my warehouses. When my people who, reckoning the period of my absence on this my seventh voyage, had found it to be seven and twenty years, and had given up all hope of me, heard of my return, they came to welcome me and to give me joy of my safety; and I related to them all that had befallen me; whereat they marvelled with exceeding marvel. Then I forswore travel and vowed to Allah the Most High I would venture no more by land or sea, for that this seventh and last voyage had surfeited me of travel and adventure; and I thanked the Lord (be He praised and glorified!), and blessed Him for having restored me to my kith and kin and country and home. "Consider, therefore, O Sindbad, O Landsman," continued Sindbad the Seaman, "what sufferings I have undergone and what perils and hardships I have endured before coming to my present state." "Allah upon thee, O my Lord!" answered Sindbad the Landsman, "pardon me the wrong I did thee." [96] And they ceased not from friendship and fellowship, abiding in all cheer and pleasures and solace of life till there came to them the Destroyer of delights and the Sunderer of Societies, and the Shatterer of palaces and the Caterer for Cemeteries to wit, the Cup of Death, and glory be to the Living One who dieth not!" [97]

ENDNOTES

SINDBAD THE SEAMAN AND SINDBAD THE LANDSMAN

[1] Lane (vol. iii. 1) calls our old friend "Es-Sindibád of the Sea," and Benfey derives the name from the Sanskrit "Siddhapati" = lord of sages. The etymology (in Heb. Sandabar and in Greek Syntipas) is still uncertain, although the term often occurs in Arab stories; and some look upon it as a mere corruption of "Bidpai" (Bidyápati). The derivation offered by Hole (*Remarks on the Arabian Nights' Entertainments*, by Richard Hole, LL.D. London, Cadell, 1797) from the Persian ábád (a region) is impossible. It is, however, not a little curious that this purely Persian word (= a "habitation") should be found in Indian names as early as Alexander's day, *e.g.*, the "Dachina bades" of the Periplus is "Dakhsin-ábád," the Sanskr. being "Dakshinapatha."
[2] A porter like the famous Armenians of Constantinople. Some edits. call him "Al-Hindibád."
[3] Arab. "Karawán" (Charadrius œdicnemus, Linn.): its shrill note is admired by Egyptians and hated by sportsmen.
[4] This ejaculation, still popular, averts the evil eye. In describing Sindbad the Seaman the Arab writer seems to repeat what one reads of Marco Polo returned to Venice.

FIRST VOYAGE OF SINDBAD THE SEAMAN

[5] Our old friend must not be confounded with the eponym of the "Sindibád-námah;" the Persian book of Sindbad the Sage.
[6] The first and second are from *Eccles*. chap. vii. 1, and ix. 4. The Bul. Edit. reads for the third, "The grave is better than the palace." None are from Solomon, but Easterns do not "verify quotations."
[7] Arab. "Kánún"; a furnace, a brasier before noticed (vol. v., p. 272); here a pot full of charcoal sunk in the ground, or a little hearth of clay shaped like a horseshoe and opening down wind.
[8] These fish-islands are common in the Classics, *e.g.*, the Pristis of Pliny (xvii. 4), which Olaus Magnus transfers to the Baltic (xxi. 6) and makes timid as the whales of Nearchus. C. J. Solinus (*Plinii Simia*) says, "Indica maria balænas habent ultra spatia quatuor jugerum." See also Bochart's *Hierozoicon* (i. 50) for Job's Leviathan (xli. 16-17). Hence deemed an island. A basking whale would readily suggest the Krakan and Cetus of Olaus Magnus (xxi.

25). Al-Kazwíni's famous treatise on the "Wonders of the World" (Ajáib al-Makhlúkát) tells the same tale of the "Sulahfah" tortoise, the colossochelys, for which see the Third Voyage of Sindbad.

[9] Sindbad does not say that he was a shipwrecked man, being a model in the matter of "travellers' tales," *i.e.*, he always tells the truth when an untruth would not serve him.

[10] Lane (iii. 83) would make this a corruption of the Hindu "Maharáj" = great Rajah: but it is the name of the great autumnal fête of the Guebres; a term composed of two good old Persian words "Mihr" (the sun, whence "Mithras") and "ján" = life. As will presently appear, in the days of the Just King Anushirwán, the Persians possessed Southern Arabia and East Africa south of Cape Guardafui (Jird Háfún). On the other hand, supposing the word to be a corruption of Maharaj, Sindbad may allude to the famous Narsinga kingdom in Mid-south India whose capital was Vijaya-nagar; or to any great Indian Rajah even he of Kachch (Cutch), famous in Moslem story as the Balhará (Ballaba Rais, who founded the Ballabhi era; or the Zamorin of Camoens, the Samdry Rajah of Malabar). For Mahrage, or Mihrage, see Renaudot's "Two Mohammedan Travellers of the Ninth Century." In the account of Ceylon by Wolf (English Transl. p. 168) it adjoins the "Ilhas de Cavalos" (of wild horses) to which the Dutch merchants sent their brood-mares. Sir W. Jones (*Description of Asia*, chap. ii.) makes the Arabian island Soborma or Mahráj = Borneo.

[11] Arab. "Sáis"; the well-known Anglo-Indian word for a groom or rather a "horse-keeper."

[12] Arab. "Darakah"; whence our word.

[13] The myth of mares being impregnated by the wind was known to the Classics of Europe; and the "sea-stallion" may have arisen from the Arab practice of picketing mare asses to be covered by the wild ass. Colonel J. D. Watson of the Bombay Army suggests to me that Sindbad was wrecked at the mouth of the Ran of Kachch (Cutch) and was carried in a boat to one of the Islands there formed during the rains and where the wild ass (*Equus Onager*, Khar-gadh, in Pers. Gor-khar) still breeds. This would explain the "stallions of the sea" and we find traces of the ass blood in the true Kathiawár horse, with his dun colour, barred legs and dorsal stripe.

[14] The second or warrior caste (Kshatriya), popularly supposed to have been annihilated by Battle-axe Ramá (Parashu Ráma); but several tribes of Rajputs and other races claim the honourable genealogy. Colonel Watson would explain the word by "Shakháyát" or noble Káthis (Kathiawar-men), or by "Shikári," the

professional hunter here acting as stable-groom.

[15] In Bul. Edit. "Kábil." Lane (iii. 88) supposes it to be the "Bartail" of Al-Kazwini near Borneo and quotes the Spaniard B. L. de Argensola (History of the Moluccas), who places near Banda a desert island, Poelsatton, infamous for cries, whistlings, roarings and dreadful apparitions, suggesting that it was peopled by devils (Stevens, vol. i., p. 168).

[16] Some texts substitute for this last phrase, "And the sailors say that Al-Dajjál is there." He is a manner of Moslem Antichrist, the Man of Sin *per excellentiam*, who will come in the latter days and lay waste the earth, leading 70,000 Jews, till encountered and slain by Jesus at the gate of Lud. (Sale's Essay, sect. 4.)

[17] Also from Al-Kazwini: it is an exaggerated description of the whale still common off the East African Coast. My crew was dreadfully frightened by one between Berberah and Aden. Nearchus scared away the whales in the Persian Gulf by trumpets (Strabo, lib. xv.). The owl-faced fish is unknown to me: it may perhaps be a seal or a manatee. Hole says that Father Martini, the Jesuit (seventeenth century), placed in the Canton Seas, an "animal with the head of a bird and the tail of a fish,"—a parrot-beak?

[18] The captain or master (not owner) of a ship.

[19] The kindly Moslem feeling, shown to a namesake, however humble.

THE SECOND VOYAGE OF SINDBAD THE SEAMAN

[20] A popular phrase to express utter desolation.

[21] The literature of all peoples contains this physiological perversion. Birds do not sing hymns; the song of the male is simply to call the female and when the pairing-season ends all are dumb.

[22] The older "roc." The word is Persian, with many meanings, *e.g.*, a cheek (Lalla "Rookh"); a "rook" (hero) at chess; a rhinoceros, etc. The fable world-wide of the *Wundervogel* is, as usual, founded upon fact: man remembers and combines but does not create. The Egyptian Bennu (Ti-bennu = phoenix) may have been a reminiscence of gigantic pterodactyls and other winged monsters. From the Nile the legend fabled by these Oriental "putters out or five for one" overspread the world and gave birth to the Eorosh of the Zend, whence the Pers. "Símurgh" (= the "thirty-fowl-like"), the "Bar Yuchre" of the Rabbis, the "Garuda" of the Hindus; the "Anká" ("long-neck") of the Arabs; the "Hathilinga bird," of Buddhagosha's Parables, which had the strength of five elephants;

the "Kerkes" of the Turks; the "Gryps" of the Greeks; the Russian "Norka"; the sacred dragon of the Chinese; the Japanese "Pheng" and "Kirni"; the "wise and ancient Bird" which sits upon the ash-tree yggdrasil, and the dragons, griffins, basilisks, etc. of the Middle Ages. A second basis wanting only a superstructure of exaggeration (M. Polo's Ruch had wing-feathers twelve paces long) would be the huge birds but lately killed out. Sindbad may allude to the Æpyornus of Madagascar, a gigantic ostrich whose egg contains 2.35 gallons. The late Herr Hildebrand discovered on the African coast, facing Madagascar, traces of another huge bird. Bochart (*Hierozoicon* ii. 854) notices the Avium Avis Ruch and taking the *pulli* was followed by lapidation on the part of the parent bird. A Persian illustration in Lane (iii. 90) shows the Rukh carrying off three elephants in beak and pounces with the proportions of a hawk and field mice: and the Rukh hawking at an elephant is a favourite Persian subject. It is possible that the "Twelve Knights of the Round Table" were the twelve Rukhs of Persian story. We need not go, with Faber, to the Cherubim which guarded the Paradise-gate. The curious reader will consult Dr. H. H. Wilson's Essays, edited by my learned correspondent, Dr. Rost, Librarian of the India House (vol. i. pp. 192-3).

[23] It is not easy to explain this passage unless it be a garbled allusion to the steel-plate of the diamond-cutter. Nor can we account for the wide diffusion of this tale of perils unless to enhance the value of the gem. Diamonds occur in alluvial lands mostly open and comparatively level, as in India, the Brazil and the Cape. Archbishop Epiphanius of Salamis (ob. A.D. 403) tells this story about the jacinth or ruby (Epiphanii Opera, a Petaio, Coloniæ 1682); and it was transferred to the diamond by Marco Polo (iii. 29, "of Eagles bring up diamonds") and Nicolò de Conti, whose "mountain Albenigaras" must be Vijayanagar in the kingdom of Golconda. Major Rennel places the famous mines of Pauna or Purna in a mountain-tract of more than 200 miles square to the southwest of the Jumna. Al-Kazwini locates the "Chaos" in the "Valley of the Moon amongst the mountains of Serendib" (Ceylon); the Chinese tell the same tale in the campaigns of Hulaku; and it is known in Armenia. Col. Yule (M. P. ii. 349) suggests that all these are ramifications of the legend told by Herodotus concerning the Arabs and their cinnamon (iii. 3). But whence did Herodotus borrow the tale?

[24] Sindbad correctly describes the primitive way of extracting camphor, a drug unknown to the Greeks and Romans, introduced by the Arabs and ruined in reputation by M. Raspail. The best Laurus Camphora grows in the Malay Peninsula, Sumatra and Borneo: although Marsden (Marco Polo) declares that the tree is not found South of the Equator. In the Calc. Edit. of two hundred Nights the camphor-island (or peninsula) is called "Al-Ríhah" which is the Arab name for Jericho-town.

[25] In Bul. Edit. Kazkazan: Calc. Karkaddan and others Karkand and Karkadan; the word being Persian, Karg or Kargadan; the χαρτάζυνον of Ælian (*Hist. Anim.* xvi. 21). The length of the horn (greatly exaggerated) shows that the white species is meant; and it supplies only walking-sticks. Cups are made of the black horn (a bundle of fibres) which, like Venetian glass, sweat at the touch of poison. A section of the horn is supposed to show white lines in the figure of a man, and sundry likenesses of birds; but these I never saw. The rhinoceros gives splendid sport and the African is perhaps the most dangerous of noble game. It has served to explain away and abolish the unicorn among the Scientists of Europe. But Central Africa with one voice assures us that a horse-like animal with a single erectile horn on the forehead exists. The late Dr. Baikic, of Niger fame, thoroughly believed in it and those curious on the subject will read about Abu Karn (Father of a Horn) in Preface (pp. xvi.-xviii.) of the *Voyage au Darfour*, by Mohammed ibn Oman al-Tounsy (Al-Tunisi), Paris, Duprat, 1845.

THE THIRD VOYAGE OF SINDBAD THE SEAMAN

[26] Ibn al-Wardi mentions an "Isle of Apes" in the Sea of China and Al-Idrísi places it two days' sail from Sukutra (Dwipa Sukhatra, Socotra). It is a popular error to explain the Homeric and Herodotean legend of the Pygmies by anthropoid apes. The Pygmy fable (Pygmæi Spithamai = 1 cubit = 3 spans) was, as usual, based upon fact, as the explorations of late years have proved: the dwarfs are homunculi of various tribes, the Akka, Doko, Tiki-Tiki, Wambilikimo ("two-cubit men"), the stunted race that share the central regions of Intertropical Africa with the abnormally tall peoples who speak dialects of the Great South African tongue, miscalled the "Bantu." Hole makes the Pygmies "monkeys," a word we have borrowed from the Italians (monichio à mono = ape) and quotes Ptolemy, Νῆσοι Σατυρῶν (Ape-Islands) East of Sunda.

[27] A kind of barge (Arab. Bárijah, plur. Bawárij) used on the Nile of sub-pyriform shape when seen in bird's eye. Lane translates "ears like two mortars" from the Calc. Edit.

[28] This giant is distinctly Polyphemus; but the East had giants and cyclopes of her own (*Hierozoicon* ii. 845). The Ajáib al-Hind (chap. cxxii.) makes Polyphemus copulate with the sheep. Sir John Mandeville (if such person ever existed) mentions men fifty feet high in the Indian Islands; and Al-Kazwini and Al-Idrisi transfer them to the Sea of China, a Botany Bay for monsters in general.

[29] Fire is forbidden as a punishment amongst Moslems, the idea being that it should be reserved for the next world. Hence the sailors fear the roasting more than the eating: with ours it would probably be the reverse. The Persian insult "Pidar-sokhtah" = (son of a) burnt father, is well known. I have noted the advisability of burning the Moslem's corpse under certain circumstances: otherwise the murderer may come to be canonised.

[30] Arab. "Mastabah" = the bench or form of masonry before noticed. In olden Europe benches were much more used than chairs, these being articles of luxury. So King Horne "sett him abenche;" and hence our "King's Bench" (Court).

[31] This is from the Bresl. Edit. vol. iv. 32: the Calc. Edit gives only an abstract and in the Bul. Edit. the Ogre returned "accompanied by a female, greater than he and more hideous." We cannot accept Mistress Polyphemus.

[32] This is from Al-Kazwini, who makes the serpent "wind itself round a tree or a rock, and thus break to pieces the bones of the breast in its belly."

[33] "Like a closet," in the Calc. Edit. The serpent is an exaggeration of the python which grows to an enormous size. Monstrous Ophidia are mentioned in sober history, *e.g.*, that which delayed the army of Regulus. Dr. de Lacerda, a sober and sensible Brazilian traveller, mentions his servants sitting down upon a tree-trunk in the Captaincy of San Paulo (Brazil), which began to move and proved to be a huge snake. F. M. Pinto (the Sindbad of Portugal though not so respectable) when in Sumatra takes refuge in a tree from "tigers, crocodiles, copped adders and serpents which slay men with their breath." Father Lobo in Tigre (chap. x.) was nearly killed by the poison-breath of a huge snake, and healed himself with a bezoar carried *ad hoc*. Maffæus makes the breath of crocodiles suavissimus, but that of the Malabar serpents and vipers "adeo teter ac noxius ut afflatu ipso necare perhibeantur."

[34] Arab. "Aurat": the word has been borrowed by the Hindostani jargon, and means a woman, a wife.

[35] So in Al-Idrísi and Langlès: the Bres. Edit. has "Al-Kalásitah"; and Al-Kazwini "Al-Salámit." The latter notes in it a petrifying spring which Camoens (*The Lus*. x. 104), places in Sunda, *i.e.*, Java-Minor of M. Polo. Some read Salabat-Timor, one of the Moluccas famed for sanders, cloves, cinnamon, etc. (Purchas ii. 1784.)

[36] Evidently the hippopotamus (*Pliny*, viii. 25; ix. 3 and xxiii. 11). It can hardly be the Mulaccan Tapir, as shields are not made of the hide. Hole suggests the buffalo which found its way to Egypt from India via Persia; but this would not be a speciosum miraculum.

[37] The ass-headed fish is from Pliny (ix. cap. 3): all those tales are founded upon the manatee (whose dorsal protuberance may have suggested the camel), the seal and the dugong or sea calf. I have noticed (*Zanzibar* i. 205) legends of ichthyological marvels current on the East African seaboard; and even the monsters of the Scottish waters are not all known: witness the mysterious "brigdie." See Bochart *De Cetis* i. 7; and Purchas iii. 930.

[38] The colossal tortoise is noticed by Ælian (*De Nat. Animal.* xvi. 17), by Strabo (Lib. xv.), by Pliny (ix. 10) and Diodorus Siculus (iv. 1) who had heard of a tribe of Chelonophagi. Ælian makes them 16 cubits long near Taprobane and serving as house-roofs; and others turn the shell into boats and coracles. A colossochelys was first found on the Scwalik Hills by Dr. Falconer and Major (afterwards Sir Proby) Cantley. In 1867 M. Emile Blanchard exhibited to the Académie des Sciences a monster crab from Japan 1.20 metres long (or 2.50 including legs); and other travellers have reported 4 metres. These crustacae seem never to cease growing and attain great dimensions under favourable circumstances, *i.e.* when not troubled by man.

[39] Lane suggests (iii. 97), and with some probability, that the "bird" was a nautilus; but the wild traditions concerning the barnacle-goose may perhaps have been the base of the fable. The albatross also was long supposed never to touch land. Possible the barnacle, like the barometz of Tartarean lamb, may be a survivor of the day when the animal and vegetable kingdoms had not yet branched off into different directions.

THE FOURTH VOYAGE OF SINDBAD THE SEAMAN

[40] Arab. "Zahwah," also meaning a luncheon. The five daily prayers made all Moslems take strict account of time, and their nomenclature of its division is extensive.

[41] This is the "insane herb." Davis, who visited Sumatra in 1599 (*Purchas* i. 120) speaks "of a kind of seed, whereof a little being eaten, maketh a man to turn foole, all things seeming to him to be metamorphosed." Linschoten's "Dutroa" was a poppy-like bud containing small kernels like melons which stamped and administered as a drink make a man "as if he were foolish, or out of his wits." This is Father Lobo's "Vanguini" of the Cafres, called by the Portuguese *dutro* (*Datura Stramonium*) still used by dishonest confectioners. It may be Dampier's Ganga (Ganjah) or Bang (Bhang) which he justly describes as acting differently "according to different constitutions; for some it stupefies, others it makes sleepy, others merry and some quite mad." (Harris, *Collect.* ii. 900.) Dr. Fryer also mentions Duty, Bung and Post, the Poust of Bernier, an infusion of poppy-seed.

[42] Arab. "Ghul," here an ogre, a cannibal. I cannot but regard the "Ghul of the waste" as an embodiment of the natural fear and horror which a man feels when he faces a really dangerous desert. As regards cannibalism, Al-Islam's religion of common sense freely allows it when necessary to save life, and unlike our mawkish modern sensibility, never blames those who

Alimentis talibus usi
Produxere animos.

[43] For Cannibals, see the Massagetæ of Herod (i.), the Padæi of India (iii.), and the Essedones near Mæotis (iv.); Strabo (lib. iv.) of the Luci; Pomponious Mela (iii. 7) and St. Jerome (ad Jovinum) of Scoti. M. Polo locates them in Dragvia, a kingdom of Sumatra (iii. 17), and in Angaman (the Andamanian Isles?), possibly the ten Maniolai which Ptolemy (vii.), confusing with the Nicobars, places on the Eastern side of the Bay of Bengal; and thence derives the Heraklian stone (magnet) which attracts the iron of ships (See Serapion, *De Magnete*, fol. 6, Edit. of 1479, and Brown's *Vulgar Errors*, p. 74, 6th Edit.). Mandeville finds his cannibals in Lamaray (Sumatra) and Barthema in the "Isle of Gyava" (Java). Ibn Al-Wardi and Al-Kazwini notice them in the Isle Saksar, in the

Sea of the Zanj (Zanzibar): the name is corrupted Persian "Sag-Sar" (Dogs'-heads) hence the dog-descended race of Camoens in Pegu (*The Lus*. x. 122). The Bresl. Edit. (iv. 52) calls them "Khawárij" = certain sectarians in Eastern Arabia. Needless to say that cocoa-nut oil would have no stupefying effect unless mixed with opium or datura, hemp or henbane.

[44] Black pepper is produced in the Goanese but we must go south to find the "Bilád al-Filfil" (home of pepper) *i.e.*, Malabar. The exorbitant prices demanded by Venice for this spice led directly to the discovery of The Cape route by the Portuguese; as the "Grains of Paradise" (Amomum Granum Paradisi) induced the English to explore the West African Coast.

[45] Arab. "Kazdír." Sansk. "Kastír." Gr. "Kassiteron." Lat. "Cassiteros," evidently derived from one root. The Heb. is "Badih," a substitute, an alloy. "Tanakah" is the vulg. Arab. word, a congener of the Assyrian "Anaku," and "Kala-i" is the corrupt Arab. term used in India.

[46] Our Arabian Ulysses had probably left a Penelope or two at home and finds a Calypso in this Ogygia. His modesty at the mention of womankind is notable.

[47] These are the commonplaces of Moslem consolation on such occasions: the artistic part is their contrast with the unfortunate widower's prospect.

[48] Lit. "a margin of stone, like the curb-stone of a well."

[49] I am not aware that this vivisepulture of the widower is the custom of any race, but the fable would be readily suggested by the Sati (Suttee)-rite of the Hindus. Simple vivisepulture was and is practised by many people.

[50] Because she was weaker than a man. The Bresl. Edit. however, has "a gugglet of water and five scones."

[51] The confession is made with true Eastern sang-froid and probably none of the hearers "disapproved" of the murders which saved the speaker's life.

[52] This tale is evidently taken from the escape of Aristomenes the Messenian from the pit into which he had been thrown, a fox being his guide. The Arabs in an early day were eager students of Greek literature. Hole (p. 140) noted the coincidence.

[53] Bresl. Edit. "Khwájah," our "Howajee," meaning a schoolmaster, a man of letters, a gentleman.

[54] And he does repeat at full length what the hearers must have known right well. I abridge.

[55] Island of the Bell (Arab. "Nákús" = a wooden gong used by Christians but forbidden to Moslems). "Kala" is written "Kela," "Kullah" and a variety of ways. Baron Walckenaer places it at Keydah in the Malay peninsula opposite Sumatra. Renaudot identifies it with Calabar, "somewhere about the point of Malabar."

THE FIFTH VOYAGE OF SINDBAD THE SEAMAN

[56] Islands, because Arab cosmographers love to place their *speciosa miracula* in such places.

[57] Like the companions of Ulysses who ate the sacred oxen (*Od.* xii.).

[58] So the enormous kingfisher of Lucian's *True History* (lib. ii.).

[59] This tale is borrowed from Ibn Al-Wardi, who adds that the greybeards awoke in the morning after eating the young Rukh with black hair which never turned white. The same legend is recounted by Al-Dimiri (ob. A.H. 808 = 1405-6) who was translated into Latin by Bochart (*Hierozoicon*, ii. p. 854) and quoted by Hole and Lane (iii. 103). An excellent study of Marco Polo's Rukh was made by my learned friend the late Prof. G. G. Bianconi of Bologna, "Dell'Uccello Ruc," Bologna, Gamberini, 1868. Prof. Bianconi predicted that other giant birds would be found in Madagascar on the East African Coast opposite; but he died before hearing of Hildebrand's discovery.

[60] Arab. "Izár," the earliest garb of Eastern man; and, as such preserved in the Meccan pilgrimage. The "waist-cloth" is either tucked in or kept in place by a girdle.

[61] Arab. "Líf," a succedaneum for the unclean sponge, not unknown in the "Turkish Baths" of London.

[62] The Persians have a Plinian monster called "Tasmeh-pá" = Strap-legs without bones. The "Old Man" is not an ourang-outang nor an Ifrít, as in Sayf al-Mulúk, but a jocose exaggeration of a custom prevailing in parts of Asia and especially in the African interior where the Tsetse-fly prevents the breeding of burden-beasts. Ibn Batútah tells us that in Malabar everything was borne upon men's backs. In Central Africa the kinglet rides a slave, and on ceremonious occasions mounts his Prime Minister. I have often been reduced to this style of conveyance and found man the worst imaginable riding: there is no hold and the sharpness of the shoulder-ridge soon makes the legs ache intolerably. The classicists of course find the Shaykh of the Sea in the Tritons and Nereus, and Bochart (*Hiero.* ii. 858, 880) notices the homo aquaticus, Senex Judæus and Senex Marinus. Hole (p. 151)

suggests the inevitable ourang-outang (man o' wood), one of "our humiliating copyists," and quotes "Destiny" in Scarron's comical romance (Part ii. chap. i) and "Jealousy" enfolding Rinaldo. (*O.F.* lib. 42).

[63] More literally "The Chief of the Sea (-Coast)," Shaykh being here a chief rather than an elder (eoldermann, alderman). So the "Old Man of the Mountain," famous in crusading days, was the Chief who lived on the Nusayriyah or Ansári range, a northern prolongation of the Libanus. Our "old man" of the text may have been suggested by the Koranic commentators on chap. vi. When an Infidel rises from the grave, a hideous figure meets him and says, "Why wonderest thou at my loathsomeness? I am thine Evil Deeds: thou didst ride upon me in the world and now I will ride upon thee." (Suiting the action to the words.)

[64] In parts of West Africa and especially in Gorilla-land there are many stories of women and children being carried off by apes, and all believe that the former bear issue to them. It is certain that the anthropoid ape is lustfully excited by the presence of women and I have related how at Cairo (1856) a huge cynocephalus would have raped a girl had it not been bayonetted. Young ladies who visited the Demidoff Gardens and menagerie at Florence were often scandalised by the vicious exposure of the baboons' parti-coloured persons. The female monkey equally solicits the attentions of man and I heard in India from my late friend, Mirza Ali Akbar of Bombay, that to his knowledge connection had taken place. Whether there would be issue and whether such issue would be viable are still disputed points: the produce would add another difficulty to the pseudo-science called psychology, as such mule would have only half a soul and issue by a congener would have a quarter-soul. A traveller well known to me once proposed to breed pithecoid men who might be useful as hewers of wood and drawers of water: his idea was to put the highest races of apes to the lowest of humanity. I never heard what became of his "breeding stables."

[65] Arab. "Jauz al-Hindi": our word cocoa is from the Port. "Coco," meaning a "bug" (bugbear) in allusion to its caricature of the human face, hair, eyes and mouth. I may here note that a cocoa-tree is easily climbed with a bit of rope or a handkerchief.

[66] Tomb-pictures in Egypt show tame monkeys gathering fruits and Grossier (*Description of China*, quoted by Hole and Lane) mentions a similar mode of harvesting tea by irritating the monkeys of the Middle Kingdom.

[67] Bresl. Edit. Cloves and cinnamon in those days grew in widely distant places.

[68] In pepper-plantations it is usual to set bananas (*Musa Paradisiaca*) for shading the young shrubs which bear bunches like ivy-fruit, not pods.

[69] The Bresl. Edit. has "Al-Ma'arat." Langlès calls it the Island of Al-Kamárí. See Lane, iii. 86.

[70] Insula, pro. peninsula. "Comorin" is a corrupt. of "Kanyá" (= Virgo, the goddess Durgá) and "Kumári" (a maid, a princess); from a temple of Shiva's wife: hence Ptolemy's Κῶρυ ἄχρον and near it to the N. East Κομαρὶα ἄχρον χαὶ πόλις, "Promontorium Cori quod Comorini caput insulæ vocant," says Maffæus (*Hist. Indic.* i. p. 16). In the text "Al'úd" refers to the eagle-wood (Aloekylon Agallochum) so called because spotted like the bird's plume. That of Champa (Cochin-China, mentioned in Camoens, *The Lus.* x. 129) is still famous.

[71] Arab. "Birkat" = tank, pool, reach, bight. Hence Birkat Far'aun in the Suez Gulf. (*Pilgrimage*, i. 297.)

THE SIXTH VOYAGE OF SINDBAD THE SEAMAN

[72] Probably Cape Comorin; to judge from the river, but the text names Sarandib (Ceylon Island) famous for gems. This was noticed by Marco Polo, iii. cap. 19; and ancient authors relate the same of "Taprobane."

[73] I need hardly trouble the reader with a note on pearl-fisheries: the descriptions of travellers are continuous from the days of Pliny (ix. 35), Solinus (cap. 56) and Marco Polo (iii. 23). Maximilian of Transylvania, in his narrative of Magellan's voyage (*Novus Orbis*, p. 532) says that the Celebes produce pearls big as turtle-doves' eggs; and the King of Porne (Borneo) had two unions as great as goose's eggs. Pigafetta (in *Purchas*) reduces this to hen's eggs and Sir Thomas Herbert to dove's eggs.

[74] Arab. "Anbar" pronounced "Ambar;" wherein I would derive "Ambrosia." Ambergris was long supposed to be a fossil, a vegetable which grew upon the sea-bottom or rose in springs; or a "substance produced in the water like naphtha or bitumen"(!): now it is known to be the egesta of a whale. It is found in lumps weighing several pounds upon the Zanzibar Coast and is sold at a high price, being held a potent aphrodisiac. A small hollow is drilled in the bottom of the cup and the coffee is poured upon the bit of ambergris it contains; when the oleaginous matter shows in

dots amidst the "Kaymagh" (coffee-cream), the bubbly froth which floats upon the surface and which an expert "coffee servant" distributes equally among the guests. Argensola mentions in Ceylon, "springs of liquid bitumen thicker than our oil and some of pure balsam."

[75] The tale-teller forgets that Sindbad and his companions have just ascended it; but this *inconséquence* is a characteristic of the Eastern Saga. I may note that the description of ambergris in the text tells us admirably well what it is not.

[76] This custom is alluded to by Lane (*Mod. Egypt*, ch. xv.): it is the rule of pilgrims to Meccah when too ill to walk or ride (*Pilgrimage*, i. 180). Hence all men carry their shrouds: mine, after being dipped in the Holy Water of Zemzem, was stolen from me by the rascally Somal of Berberah.

[77] Arab. "Fulk;" some Edits. read "Kalak" and "Ramaz" (= a raft).

[78] These lines occur in modified form in Night xi.

[79] These underground rivers (which Dr. Livingstone derided) are familiar to every geographer from Spenser's "Mole" to the Poika of Adelberg and the Timavo near Trieste. Hence "Peter Wilkins" borrowed his cavern which let him to Grande-volet. I have some experience of Sindbad's sorrows, having once attempted to descend the Poika on foot. The Classics had the Alpheus (*Pliny* v. 31; and Seneca, *Nat. Quae*. vi.), and the Tigris-Euphrates supposed to flow underground: and the Mediævals knew the Abana of Damascus and the Zenderúd of Isfahan.

[80] Abyssinians can hardly be called "blackamoors," but the arrogance of the white skin shows itself in Easterns (*e.g.* Turks and Brahmans) as much as, if not more than, amongst Europeans. Southern India at the time it was explored by Vasco da Gama was crowded with Abyssinian slaves imported by the Arabs.

[81] "Sarandib" and "Ceylon" (the Taprobane of Ptolemy and Diodorus Siculus) derive from the Pali "Sihalam" (not the Sansk. "Sinhala") shortened to Silam and Ilam in old Tamul. Van der Tunk would find it in the Malay "Pulo Selam" = Isle of Gems (the Ratna-dwípa or Jewel Isle of the Hindus and the Jazirat al-Yakút or Ruby-Island of the Arabs); and the learned Colonel Yule (*Marco Polo*, ii 296) remarks that we have adopted many Malayan names, *e.g.*, Pegu, China and Japan. Sarandib is clearly "Selan-dwípa," which Mandeville reduced to "Silha."

[82] This is the well-known Adam's Peak, the Jabal al-Ramun of the Arabs where Adam fell when cast out of Eden in the lowest or lunar sphere. Eve fell at Jeddah (a modern myth) and the unhappy pair met at Mount Arafat (*i.e.*, recognition) near Meccah. Thus their fall was a fall indeed. (*Pilgrimage*, iii. 259.)

[83] He is the Alcinous of our Arabian Odyssey.

[84] This word is not in the dictionaries; Hole (p. 192) and Lane understand it to mean the hog-deer; but why, one cannot imagine. The animal is neither "beautiful" nor "uncommon" and most men of my day have shot dozens in the Sind-Shikárgahs.

[85] M. Polo speaks of a ruby in Seilan (Ceylon) a palm long and three fingers thick: William of Tyre mentions a ruby weighing twelve Egyptian drams (*Gibbon* ii. 123), and Mandeville makes the King of Mammera wear about his neck a "rubye orient" one foot long by five fingers large.

[86] The fable is from Al-Kazwini and Ibn Al-Wardi who place the serpent (an animal sacred to Æsculapius, *Pliny*, xxix. 4) "in the sea of Zanj" (*i.e.* Zanzibar). In the "garrow hills" of N. Eastern Bengal the skin of the snake Burrawar (?) is held to cure pain. (*Asiat. Res.* vol. iii.)

[87] For "Emerald," Hole (p. 177) would read emery or adamantine spar.

[88] Evidently Maháráj = Great Rajah, Rajah in Chief, an Hindu title common to the three potentates before alluded to, the Narsinga, Balhara or Samiry.

[89] This is probably classical. So the page said to Philip of Macedon every morning, "Remember, Philip, thou art mortal"; also the slave in the Roman Triumph,

"Respice poste te: hominem te esse memento!"

And the dying Severus, "Urnlet, soon shalt thou enclose what hardly a whole world could contain." But the custom may also have been Indian: the contrast of external pomp with the real vanity of human life suggests itself to all.

THE SEVENTH VOYAGE OF SINDBAD THE SEAMAN

[90] Arab. "Hút"; a term applied to Jonah's whale and to monsters of the deep, "Samak" being the common fishes.

[91] Usually a two-bow prayer.

[92] This is the recognised formula of Moslem sales.

[93] Arab. "Walímah"; like our wedding-breakfast but a much more ceremonious and important affair.

[94] *i.e.*, his wife (euphemistically). I remember an Italian lady being much hurt when a Maltese said to her "Mia moglie—con rispetto parlando" (my wife, saving your presence). "What," she cried, "he speaks of his wife as he would of the sweepings!"

[95] The serpent in Arabic is mostly feminine.

[96] *i.e.*, in envying his wealth, with the risk of the evil eye.

[97] I subjoin a translation of the Seventh Voyage from the Calc. Edit. of the two hundred Nights which differs in essential points from the above. All respecting Sindbad the Seaman has an especial interest. In one point this world-famous tale is badly ordered. The most exciting adventures are the earliest and the falling off of the interest has a somewhat depressing effect. The Rukh, the Ogre and the Old Man o' the Sea should come last.

THE END